This book is dedicated to the memory of my three wonderful sisters. I love and miss you every day. X

Contents

Chapter 1: Home Sweet Home

What a prospect! Another Monday! Another week! Still, only two more and it would be half-term. Usually I found it hard to wake up, especially on a Monday, but today it seemed different. Ever since a cat had kicked off a dustbin lid at half past five and startled me awake, I just lay there, hands behind head, in the half-light of my tiny box bedroom.

I was trying to decide what the damp patch on the corner of the ceiling above the window reminded me of. I had watched with interest over the last few months the steady growth of the yellowish fungus and wondered how long it would be before the useless council would do something about it.

My name is Brian Paul Wilson. I am fourteen years old and live in complete frustration with my formidable mother, Joyce, and my three older, overweight sisters – Gloria, Brenda and Hilary.

My father, Kenneth Arthur Wilson, was a slightly built, weasel-featured, pathetic excuse of a man. The concept of love and family values were way above his self-centred comprehension. He selfishly never got to grips with his responsibilities and seriously attempted to provide for his family.

Ten years earlier, without a second thought or pang of guilt, he turned his back on any semblance of normal life when he ditched his steady plumbing job to follow his dream and become a self-employed sign writer and artist. His undoubted flair for anything arty was completely wasted on Mum, as she constantly struggled to make ends meet with his meagre and sporadic financial contributions to the housekeeping pot.

Back last summer the tension and constant rows reached boiling point and one sunny July morning, when Mum was busy in the kitchen and the rest of us were out of the house, Dad had collected a few items of clothing from his wardrobe and silently disappeared off the face of the earth.

Far from being devastated by his departure, Mum was ecstatic and visibly heaving many sighs of relief. At least now she would be entitled to social security payments and a regular weekly amount coming into the house to live on. Heaven!

Mother was a kindly sort and since our dad

had done a bunk, she had thrown herself into caring for me, almost to suffocation point. For a lot of the time I enjoyed the pampering, but for the rest of the time I desperately craved my independence and to be allowed to do what other lads of my age do, such as going to the park or hanging around on street corners with me mates. It always amazes me that I could catch the bus and travel three miles to school and yet my mother wouldn't trust me two hundred yards up the road to the park.

Joyce Marjorie Wilson gave birth to me at the grand old age of forty-six, and coming into a declining marriage, my early years were crammed full of unhealthy influences. Although I was straightaway placed on a pedestal, by both my dear old mum and my old-fashioned sisters, most of my fears and anxieties stemmed from them, and the embarrassing poverty-stricken life that I endured.

Sometimes the sense of insecurity and not knowing how to break the mould of family traditions and ties seemed impossible. Often, in the past, my frustrations had manifested themselves as violent tantrums. Many of my teachers had found me quite uncontrollable and I'd either received a kick or a punch whilst I freaked out in one of my black moods. My frustrations nowadays appeared as long depressions and a sad, hollow feeling of hopelessness.

I appeared to be reaching puberty clumsily through the back door. The only noticeable body changes I had to date was a line of juicy pimples along the crease of my chin and a nose that was growing faster than the rest of my face.

Bristol was a gloomy place this time of year. In fact, in the area that we lived it was very drab and depressing all year round. Home was a grotty Victorian council house, with three up and two down, in one of the poorest districts of town.

On this bleak February morning, I decided to do something spontaneous and right out of my boring routine. I would actually get up before my mother's melodic tones would echo up the stairs. "Brian! Are you getting up? It's half-past seven." Her broad Bristolian accent really made her sound classy.

That's it, I'm getting up, I thought. And in one movement I pulled back the rough blankets and stumbled to my feet. The cold room felt musty. I moved unsteadily to the window, held the moth-eaten curtain back with one hand, and wiped the freezing condensation from the glass with the other, trying to focus on the obscure view. All I could see was dirty, red-bricked terraced houses, all with their own scruffy concrete backyards, all looking just as ugly as they did yesterday. *Morning world*, I whispered, still with the gruffness of eight hours' sleep in my throat.

As my body and soul slowly clicked together, I realised that I was bursting for my first pee of the day, so I yanked open the creaky door and scurried gingerly along the icy lino to the bathroom. Bathroom. That makes it sound posh! And it certainly was anything but. The deep white chipped bath was badly stained brown and books held up one of the corners since one of the claw-shaped feet had rotted away. The prehistoric gas heater standing menacingly above the bath dominated half of the flaking magnolia wall. If you were desperate enough to attempt a bath, you literally took your life into your own hands when trying to light the pilot with a strip of flaming newspaper. My eyebrows had only just grown back after my last bath. I pulled the string light switch and with a clunk, on came the unshaded sixty-watt bulb.

I was about ten seconds into my "widdle" before noticing that I had left the dark wooden seat down. I tutted loudly to myself. This meant another job. If I didn't wipe my splashes off my mother would delight in giving me a lecture on how I was a lazy git and I didn't deserve a bloody thing.

"Brian! Are you getting up? It's half-past seven."

Oh no. I had hoped to have got downstairs before my mum's alarm call. Now everything was ruined. I was forced to face up to the fact that it was just another ordinary day.

"Okay, Mum. I'm already up!"

"Well, don't hog that bathroom. You know how our Gloria likes to hurry on a morning."

I wonder if Prince Charles was embarrassed by his mother when he was fourteen. I doubt it.

I smiled as I wiped the seat, pulled the toilet chain and farted as I moved to study myself in the dusty cabinet mirror. Why do some people look good in the mornings, yet I always have creases down my face that were usually visible until at least ten o'clock. Oh yes, today was a particularly good day. My hair was also sticking up like a duck's arse. I don't know why I bother.

Chapter 2: School Days

Southleaze Comprehensive is a large twenty-five-year-old school situated in the middle of a huge housing estate that was built about the same time. Up until recently the school had enjoyed a good reputation for discipline and academic standards.

Two of my cousins had attended Southleaze years earlier and on the recommendation of her sister, Mother applied. Because of the family link, and after a gruelling interview with the headmaster, Mr Longton, I was given a place. There was no doubt that everything about the school was an improvement on the ones local to my home, but being the only one starting from Downton Primary, the first few months were very lonely as I tried to make a completely new set of friends.

It was probably the main reason why I struck up such a close relationship with Philip Morgan. His situation was very similar to mine as he had just moved to Bristol from South Wales. Mum hated Philip, but that didn't matter much because she never took to any of my pals. For that matter, she never had time for any of my sisters' friends either. I believed that this was because she had an enlarged over-protective gland which gave her a primitive intolerance of anyone else's offspring. Usually her reasons for disliking were really obscure. Philip's eyes were too close together, which made him a criminal. That was his downfall. That and his grating Welsh accent, that was a fatal combination.

I was still hopelessly trying to comb my hair down as I walked towards the school. Most of the other school-bound pupils were wearing the latest fashions, either a Crombie or ex-army overcoat, but not poor old me. I must have been the only prat in England still sporting a duffle coat. I know it's not my mum's fault. Money was always very tight, but it meant that I was inevitably three steps behind what was Mod. 1971 was certainly a terrible time to be a teenager if you were poverty-stricken.

"Hello Ringo!" shouted a spotty youth as he cycled past.

"Very funny," I murmured.

I know only too well that the wisecrack was a jibe at my long hair. Ironic, isn't it? I had harped the life out of my Mother for months for a Beatles-style haircut and the week that I finally got my way, everyone else in the world turned into a skinhead. Bloody typical!

I pushed my rucksack safer onto my shoulder and plunged my hands deeper into my duffle coat pockets.

One more embarrassment to overcome and I could start to enjoy my day. It was the same every Monday. Who invented the school dinner ticket system? They want sodding shooting! There were two queues of pupils of various shapes and sizes heading towards the school hall. The longer line was made up of normal children, those who actually paid for their school meals. They were issued with the yellow tickets. I had to stand with the poor unfortunates, those, who for one reason or another, had only to state their name to be given a free blue ticket. For ninety percent of the time you could bluff and lie about who and what you were, but this was such a declaration of poverty it really hurt. I always tried to time it so there was none of my mates about, but it was impossible. So, then my plan two would come into operation. When asked why I didn't pay for my dinners I would always make up stories, like my dad's an out-of-work actor or we're waiting for a large inheritance to come through. No one ever believed my fibs, but I lived in hope.

After an extended registration period, due to a

false alarm fire bell, the pupils scattered their many ways to their first lessons. For me it was English, with Mrs Wobbletits Walker. The big rumour of the moment was that the well-endowed Mrs Walker was leaning over a first year, had leant a bit too far, and her left one had fallen out knocking over an ink well. I could do a good impression of the way she would wobble into a classroom. My desk was in the second row, right in line with the teacher. There was an empty seat beside me because Philip Morgan was off with the whooping cough.

"Start reading page six from your Wuthering Heights books," rattled Mrs Walker, and without an explanation she stood up and waddled out of the classroom.

No sooner had the door shut behind her when a girl from the back of the classroom shouted, "Go on, Brian! Take over for her!" I slowly and deliberately pulled myself to my feet. I pushed my fist-clenched hands up the front of my jumper and stuck out my arse. The whole class erupted into wild laughter and clapped frantically as I became intoxicated with my success. I waddled to the front of the classroom, stood behind the teacher's desk and proceeded to make my makeshift tits dance as I whistled the Sailor's Hornpipe.

So oblivious was I to all around me that I didn't even notice the plump figure of Mrs Walker tiptoe back into the room. I carried on whistling and dancing disrespectfully. It was only the sharp blow from the enraged teacher on my ear that abruptly brought me back to my senses. I hastily stopped my mimicry, lowered my head and kept as a low a profile as possible as I blushed back to my seat.

Mrs Walker's face was purple to bursting point. She found her voice. "Right you lot. Simmer down. And as for you, Mike Yarwood, you're in detention tonight."

I gazed aimlessly at the floor, trembling with a combination of fear and total confusion, with my left ear glowing like a furnace.

After a while things started to settle down a bit and I began to reflect on the events of the last few minutes. I kicked myself for my stupidity. Not another sodding detention! I didn't mind the extra work it involved, but the worry it caused for my overbearing mother. She always threw a wobbler when I was late home from school. Her plump apron-clad figure would be waiting at the front door, arms outstretched, bellowing uncontrollably.

The rest of the day passed quite uneventfully and as I arrived home at twenty past five, more than an hour later than usual, as predicted my mum, fraught with concern, ran, as well as her portly frame would allow, to greet me in floods of tears.

"Where's been, my love?" she wailed, swamping me in a vice-like grip.

"Oh, um, I had a football meeting," I lied.

Well, I didn't want the world knowing my business, did I?

After I had finished my tea, I half-heartedly did my homework before taking my place perched on a rickety wicker stool in the decaying and gloomy back room, three feet away from the smelly paraffin heater and six feet from the large television that balanced unsteadily on an old wooden coffee table.

"What was your football meeting about then, son?" enquired Mum, as she manoeuvred her formidable bum onto the sofa to the side of the huge aspidistra plant.

"Oh, we've got a match tomorrow after school." Good thinking Brian, because at least that much was true and gave a slither of credibility to the story.

"Good job I asked you then, weren't it, or I wouldn't have known you'd be late home tomorrow as well."

"Yes you would!" I snapped back. "I was going to get you to clean my boots."

"You cheeky git!" replied Mum with a broad smile changing her mood. "I can't stay mad with you long can I?"

Isn't it bloody marvellous, I thought, she can't even recognise when I'm trying to be disrespectful to her. I just can't win.

Chapter 3: My Football Boots

Match days are always good days. I knew that I had to stay out of trouble with the teachers. I couldn't risk getting a detention that night, otherwise I would miss the game.

Since starting at my senior school, I had discovered a natural talent for all sports, particularly athletics and football. I finally had found an outlet for my many frustrations and my inferiority complex. I was now capable of shutting off from the real world for short periods of time and enjoying the calming effect of physical endeavour. I shamefully kept my family completely in the dark about my sporting prowess and achievements, not wanting them to somehow ruin things, as they always did if things looked to be going well for me.

As I rammed my football kit into a large brown carrier bag, I was blissfully unaware of just how well the day was about to unfold in front of me.

"Mum! Where's my football boots?" I shouted.

"I don't ruddy know! Don't ask me," retorted Mum.

"Oh no! I'll be late if I got to hunt for them," I squealed.

"Here's your old'uns, son," said Mum, placing another bag on the pale green kitchen table.

I held my head in my hands and sighed. "No way! I can't wear there bloody stupid things. I'll be a laughing stock."

"Well, it's they or nothin'," snorted Mum, growing rapidly impatient at the attitude of her ungrateful son.

She picked up a piece of limp cold toast and rammed it quite unceremoniously into her toothless mouth. She pulled savagely at it until the rubbery bread ripped and then, as ungainly as you like, chomped and chomped looking for all the world as if she was performing in a gurning contest as her nose and chin met repeatedly.

I was still cursing as I waited at the bus stop, just fifty yards along the road from my home. How can I wear these bloody Stanley Matthews efforts? What a big laugh for me team mates. They'll all have their modern six-studded boots and I have to wear the ones that cost our mum threepence at a church jumble sale. I had been forced to wear them once before to a practice match, but reluctantly had to quit after just ten minutes as mud seemed to be magnetically attracted to these over-the-ankle clodhoppers. Not only did I become two stone heavier, but a good six inches taller. I gazed up at the dismal grey sky. Although it was icy cold, it was dry. Please God, don't let it rain, and it might just save me from making a tit of myself.

By the time I reached the school gates my feet and cheeks were as cold as stone. I wiped my nose with the back of my black leather-effect gloved hand and to my surprise I found that it left a wet trail along my thumb and forefinger. Swiftly I slid my hand down my coat and quickened my step to a trot as the bell signifying the start of the school day rang out.

After placing my old duffle coat and carrier bag into my metal locker, I hurried along the tunnel-shaped corridor towards my form room. I vigorously stretched my mouth repeatedly in all directions, still trying to get the feeling back into my face after the biting cold air.

Chapter 4: Love's Young Dream

The main school hall at Southleaze was a large, single-storey building that had been added to the main body of the school five years earlier. Three sets of double doors cleverly linked it to the existing corridors. This multi-function space, with its floor-to-ceiling glass on two sides, served as dining hall, exams room, and venue for the many shows and concerts put on through the year. An impressive three feet high stage adorned the far wall, elegantly framed with heavy crimson velvet curtains and a large black painted pelmet.

Tuesday mornings meant assembly. The one time in the week when all twelve hundred Southleaze pupils were crammed uncomfortably together for worship.

Vernon Longton, the humourless head teacher, had already taken up his usual pose standing high above the noisy incoming mob, right in the middle of the imposing wooden platform. The stocky fifty-seven-year-old, with his short receding grey hair, impatiently shifted his formidable frame from one foot to the other, his heavy jowls rhythmically twitching as his face contorted into a menacing scowl. He awkwardly folded his arms across his blue-suited chest.

Thirty years earlier he had embarked on his career, as most teachers do, with a driving passion for making a difference to young people's lives. As the years had worn on, his optimism and energy had been systematically drained from him, as general standards of discipline and behaviour levels had slowly but surely plummeted. His enjoyment and energy for mentoring was now replaced with a resentment and a feeling of utter contempt for the juveniles that were entrusted to his care. Retirement now couldn't come quick enough for this disillusioned tutor. He had had enough of trying to "educate pork".

Once the unruly mob, comprising of various sizes, shapes and colours, had found their spot and simmered down to a semblance of order, they were subjected to a few well-chosen words of wisdom and spiritual guidance from the unfeeling head teacher. This was followed by a short prayer and a badly sung hymn. It hardly seemed worth all the effort to pack this disinterested throng of reprobates into assembly just for ten minutes of scratching and yawning, before being herded line by line back into the corridors and off to their first lessons.

Geography was first on my timetable today. As I weaved precariously through the chaos of over a thousand youngsters mindlessly darting this way and that, I spotted just in front of me two of my nutty classmates, Geoff Robinson and Steve Hawkham.

"That homework was a bit salty last night, wasn't it?" were my first words, glancing from one boy to another.

Geoff, a short tubby boy with coarse ginger hair, was first to react. "What you on about, Bri? It was a piece of piss!"

"Yes, bloody easy!" added the taller blonde lad.

They both turned and strutted away with an unconvincing arrogant swagger.

"You pair of prats!" I shouted.

Geoff instinctively turned and blew a loud raspberry as he thrust his hand into the air into a V-sign.

They moved away, still trying to look cool. I smiled, checked that my eyes didn't have any sleep in them with my thumb and forefinger, and then scampered after my comical pals.

We arrived at room two just as everyone else did. Everyone pushed and shoved four at a time through the door and in a few seconds, after much chair scraping and desk banging, we were all ready for the arrival of Mr "Beaky" Rosewall, or "Snozzle" as he was sometimes affectionately known.

The unfortunate Mr Rosewall was a happy-go-lucky chap that must have done something really dreadful in a past life, because in this one he had been forced to live with the biggest hook-shaped nose I had ever seen. It dominated and seemed to consume the rest of his swarthy features.

After a short while he staggered in juggling a stack of books in his right hand and a well-worn leather brief case in the other. Simon Parker, the class genius and chief creep-ass, was up and out of his seat in a flash hurrying to assist the struggling teacher. He relieved Snozzle of four books and placed them onto the desk.

"Thank you, Simon, very thoughtful of you," barked Mr Rosewall.

Simon Parker returned to his seat, walking with an air of superiority. The class spontaneously chanted 'Teacher's pet! Teacher's pet!' This was a well-rehearsed jibe at Simon who was always giving his classmates occasion to cringe at his virtuous actions.

"All right you lot, shut your faces!" shouted Snozzle. "It's a pity more of you aren't so thoughtful."

I glanced round at Simon Parker, who was sitting with his arms neatly folded, with a self-satisfied smirk perched on his heavily freckled face.

Oh I'd like to . . . my thoughts were interrupted by the teacher's loud voice booming across the room. "Wilson! Turn around and keep quiet."

I heard the knock on the classroom door, but chose not to glance up from my reading, engrossed as I was in the crop rotation of the Tundra Valley.

The voice of Mr Rosewall finally broke my concentration. "Class, stop reading and pay attention."

I reluctantly lifted my head from my text book and in a matter of seconds I knew that my life would never be the same again, for standing not more than two yards in front of me, next to the overweight teacher, stood a vision of loveliness. Who was she? I stared uncontrollably at this pretty blonde-haired girl. I knew I was drooling but I didn't care. I was also aware that my jaw had dropped feebly. I tried to close my mouth, but it was impossible. My trance made me forget what muscles were necessary to bring my lips together, so I just sat there gawping and dribbling copiously onto my exercise book.

"This is Diane Lewis," said Mr Rosewall.

I half took in his words, but was more intent on keeping my eyes fixed on the most beautiful thing I had ever seen. *You're untrue,* I thought. *Your hair is so beautiful, your figure so perfect, your skin so soft, your eyes so blue.* I couldn't understand my own feelings.

I had never before been interested in girls like this and my only experience of sex happened four months earlier in the gym during a games lesson. As I climbed and strained to ascend a rope, my groin repeatedly came into contact with the rough twine. By the time I had reached the ceiling of the gym I was in ecstasy and clung on tight as a pulsating thrill shuddered through my whole body.

"What the bloody hell are you doing, Wilson?" bellowed Mr Smith, the bemused games master, as he and twenty boys stood below gazing upwards at this lone figure of me cuddling into my first love.

A few nights later I had had a vivid dream in which I married the rope.

I could see myself standing at the alter and the vicar was chanting, "Do you Brian Wilson take this piece of rope to be your lawful wedded wife?"

"I do," I said proudly.

"Wilson! Shut your gob, there's a train coming!" I managed to close my mouth enough to compose myself a little. My throat was unusually dry due to the length of time that it had been dangling open. I swallowed hard several times to make it moisten again.

"As I was saying, this is Diane Lewis," Mr Rosewall continued. "Her family have just moved into the area and Diane will be joining this class. Please try to make her feel at home." *Oh, just give us a chance*, I thought, still completely mesmerised by this fourteen-year-old, five foot tall beauty.

Mr Rosewall smiled warmly at her and she reacted with a cute grin. All this attention was starting to affect her and her porcelain complexion turned to a bright pink. *Oh, she's sensitive as well*, I thought. *Isn't that lovely!* Beaky Rosewall recognised the girl's growing embarrassment and tried to lighten the mood and of course it had to be at my expense.

"I know that it's your first day, and I hate to inflict a fate that's worse than death on you, but can you see that ugly-looking youth in the second row? Just for now, d'you think you could sit by him? I know he looks 'horrible, but he's "harmless really."

He finished to the laughter of the class.

Thank you, you fat git, I muttered under my breath. That's just the introduction I was hoping for. Diane looked at me, smiled and nodded as she walked towards me. *She's not laughing, she's smiling at I*, I thought. All the hairs on the back of my neck stood on end as she elegantly took her place alongside me.

"Pleased to meet you, Brian," she whispered.

My stomach turned over as more emotions flooded through me.

I floated through the rest of the day with just one person occupying my thoughts. The gorgeous Diane Lewis.

Chapter 5: Bad Impressions

The school was split into four houses and Graham Smith was my housemaster. At thirty-two he was one of the youngest that the school had ever had. He was popular with the boys as he was one of the few teachers that treated them like human beings and didn't talk down to them. Unmistakably a games master, his six-foot ginger-haired frame always encased in a tracksuit and trainers, and always looking as if he had just undertaken violent exercise on account of his ruddy complexion. He was very proud of his footballers at the school, especially the third-year team who were as yet unbeaten.

"I've some good news and some bad news," said Mr Smith as he placed a bulging black sack onto the rickety old bench at the end of the changing rooms.

"Oh ah, what`s that then, Sir?" asked Dave Berret, who was sitting on his hands next to me.

"Well, it's like this lads," he went on. "You know I promised you that you'd all have new kit for this game?"

All the boys in unison said, "Yeah?"

"Well you have got new kit, but I think that

you might be a teeny-weeny bit disappointed with it."

Once again came the chorus, "Yeah?"

"Mr Longton decided it best to buy a set of kit that would fit you lot, the fourth, the fifth, and the sixth years."

As he finished he plunged his hands into the black sack and produced a selection of bright red shirts, shorts and socks. He started throwing one of each to all the boys. As each lad caught their own kit, they held them up against them to assess the size.

"Bloody Nora!"

"Kiss my ass!"

"What's think I am? Bloody Billy Bunter?" was typical of the many comments hurtling around the room.

The only good thing about it was that they were so pre-occupied with the voluminous kit that there wasn't any reaction to my threepenny football boots. I turned over the cuffs of my shirt five times before my hands were visible, tucked the two feet of excess shirt into my huge shorts, pulled them up high and rolled the waistband over twice. Then I strutted out of the changing room with my Max Wall-style walk and went on towards the sports field. "George Best, eat your heart out!" I shouted, breaking into a run to catch up with the others who were making their way towards the lined pitch. The opposing team were already there merrily kicking their rough-looking practice balls to one another. I heard the sniggers and wisecracks about the new kit as I trotted past and onto the pitch. *That's it*, I thought, *I'll make 'em suffer for taking the piss!*

Large areas of the pitch had little or no grass through over-use, but fortunately for me the bare patches were hard through the lack of rain. I took my usual place on the left wing and right from the start looked every inch an accomplished player. Each touch of the ball was sure and imaginative and when I received a good pass ten minutes into the game, I calmly walked the ball around the despairing keeper and blasted it into the net. I just managed to hear Mr Smith yell excitedly, "Well done, my beauty!" as I was mobbed by my ecstatic teammates. I scored once more and made another goal for my fellow striker, Terry Davis, before half-time. Then, with a mighty shrill, the referee blew his whistle and Graham Smith started applauding as his team made their way towards him at the centre line. He handed a slice of orange to each player as they reached him. He congratulated everybody in turn on their performance.

"Well done, Brian!" he beamed. "That's the

best I've ever seen you play. Carry on like that, son, and I'll get you a trial for Rovers & City."

"Cheers, Sir," I said, devouring my sour orange with a grimace.

We started the second half as we had finished the first and passed the football around with skill and authority. When the ball ran out of play I ambled off the pitch towards the school after it. I noticed a group walking towards me and as I bent down to pick up the ball, glanced up and was able to make out that one of the six girls was Diane Lewis. I remained completely motionless as I stared at her.

"Hurry up!" shouted Mr Smith impatiently.

I turned on my heels and sprinted back to the pitch. I kept casting a glance in her direction and was pleased to discover that the group were heading my way to watch the remainder of the match. *What an opportunity*, I thought. *This is my chance to impress and she couldn't have picked a better game to watch me.*

All went well for a few minutes and it wasn't until the ball went out of play that I noticed a chilly wind suddenly spring up from nowhere. The sky quickly darkened, thunder grumbled in the distance and big spots of rain began to descend on my upturned face. *I don't bloody believe it!* I howled. *Thank you, God! Thank you!*

All six girls had umbrellas and I watched through the drizzle as Diane put up a snazzy-looking see-through brolly and positioned it elegantly above her head. I tried to ignore the rain as long as my boots would allow, but the torrent was getting steadily harder. Within sixty seconds the rock hard playing surface was changed to a soggy paddy field. However hard I concentrated on what I was doing, fate was about to deal me another kick in the goolies. The world-beating winger of the first half had now turned into a Norman Wisdom lookalike. It felt like wading through porridge as I made one attempt after another to keep my feet. *What a sod!* I cursed as I dragged my pathetic figure once again from the mud. I got to my knees and looked over to the touch line. My newly-found infatuation was still there and through all of this disgrace I took time to feast my eyes on the only girl in the world that I would gladly die for. We still somehow managed to scrape together a victory of three-two, the final whistle eventually saving me from more degradation, but enough damage had been done, I felt. I had precious little chance with the girl I adored, but now how could I ever face her again?

"Don't forget to take your boots off before you get into the changing rooms," barked Mr Smith as the steaming drowned rats approached the concrete area between the fence, the tennis courts and the school. We all stopped outside the door and attempted to remove our footwear. The task was ten times harder for me. I scraped the thick cold mud from the bottom of my boots and fought with the sodden laces. By this time the rest of the boys had finished and were gingerly walking back into the warmth of the changing room, leaving me still tugging in desperation at the stubborn knots. I sensed someone watching me and as I looked was amazed to see just a few yards away from me Diane looking more enchanting than ever. We looked at each other for some time before the sumptuous lass broke the silence.

"Thank you for helping me through my first day, Brian."

With jumbled feelings I tried unsteadily to rise to my feet and before I could engineer an adequate response my feet had yet again betrayed me, sliding from underneath me like two banana skins and I landed with a thud on my backside. Not knowing whether to laugh or cry with embarrassment surging through me, and not knowing quite how to deal with this situation.

"You really are a clown!" smiled Diane as she slowly walked away.

As Diane trudged wearily through the school grounds she frowned, reflecting on her strange existence thus far.

Her father Paul was a fully qualified chartered accountant. He was highly intelligent and from an early age was expected to achieve great things in his chosen profession. He had moved away from his home at nineteen-years-old to go to university and whilst there met and quickly married Sally, a fashion model, who was incredibly attractive, but was as thick as two short planks. There was no need for them to be compatible as Father lived and breathed his work and had no real need for normal companionship of marriage.

Sally was quite content as long as Paul could keep her in the manner to which she had been accustomed during her ultra-successful career.

Soon after he had obtained his degree with honours, Paul started work for a national audit company. Until a regional post became vacant in the firm, he would be part of the troubleshooting team sorting out problems for businesses the length and breadth of Britain.

Diane was born in Leeds, but since the age of ten had lived for six months at a time in most of the major cities in the British Isles. Her own life was almost that of a travelling circus troupe, without the excitement of the Big Top and the other families to strike up relationships with.

Like Brian she was completely dissatisfied with her lot and very lonely. She had never wanted for anything materially, but yearned desperately for a close friend other than the scores of pen pals she had accumulated from her shallow acquaintances struck up along the way. Her wealthy parents required her to fit rigidly into their plastic existence and living up to their exacting expectations was becoming more and more of a heavier burden to bear. She would gladly have given up her got-it-all image for some down-to-earth, family love and a hint of humour in her fickle life. At last in Bristol her father had a permanent position and she, for the first time, had a front door to call her own. This was an opportunity to become a normal teenager.

She smiled as she thought of Brian's antics and started to feel a deep affinity with him, never before experienced. Diane loved his apparent natural popularity and his light-hearted sincerity. She also saw in him a grasp of normal living, unknown by herself. In her own way she thought herself as far removed and unacceptable as he did to her.

I watched until she was out of sight. By the time I had made the changing room it was empty. Laughter and singing came from behind the steamy partition in the corner as the team showered. Now in the warm room I proceeded to divest myself of the clinging shirt, pulling out the masses of material. I managed to get it free and with a splat it hit the changing room floor. I stood up and then suddenly realised that something was stirring within my shorts. *What the 'ell's happening to me?* I thought. Yesterday it was my jaw I couldn't control and now it's my fisherman's friend struggling to make a bid for freedom out of the top of my pants.

Mr Smith walked through. "Don't forget school rules, Wilson, you must have a shower."

I began to panic. I knew that I couldn't get out of having a wash, but how could I? One by one the other boys emerged from behind the partition and with lots of giggling and chatter proceeded to dry themselves.

The sports teacher once again appeared.

"Wilson! Shower!" he ordered.

I reluctantly peeled down my pants and as I did so, cupped my left hand over my rising predicament. I grabbed a towel and dived for the shower. The rest of the team seemed not to notice, apart from Ian Seymour.

"Sir, Sir, Sir!" he whined as he grabbed the flimsy material from around my middle.

"What is it, Seymour?" barked Mr Smith from his changing room.

"Sir, Sir, Brian's got the hard on!"

Chapter 6: Brian's Song

"Oh Gloria! I have never seen you look as radiant as you do tonight," I mocked, pushing shut the front door behind me.

"Get stuffed you cheeky little toe rag," rebuked Gloria as she carried on preening herself in the full-length mirror at the bottom of the stairs.

"That's not very nice, is it, you gorgeous hunk of womanhood!" I smarmed.

"Sod off!" she continued. "You can't even wait 'til you've shut the front door before you start, can you?"

"Yes I can. The front door was definitely shut."

Gloria just grunted and continued to backcomb her shoulder-length mousy hair.

"What are you all dolled up for Glor anyhow?" I said. "There was a full moon last week, or are you going out chasing they Land Rovers again?"

"I'll bloody lam you one in a minute," declared the enraged, overweight seventeen-year-old.

I decided that I had pushed her far enough this time with the wisecracks as my older sister was not averse to dishing out corporal punishment. There was plenty of room to pass behind her in the hallway but I made a meal of it, pretending to have difficulty getting by.

After flopping my sodden overcoat over the banister, I made for the kitchen. Within the confines of the cosy room, I began to feel some regret for teasing my sister, but I could never resist an opportunity.

In many ways our love/hate relationship was typical of many brothers and sisters. We would defend each other to all and sundry, but there was never a civil word spoken between us.

Mum and my other two sisters were sitting around the kitchen table drinking tea. Brenda and Hilary were twenty-four and twenty-six-years-old respectively and being that much older always treated me with more of a motherly approach. Brenda had auburn hair, whilst Hilary had dyed black. They both sported unnatural-looking buns on top of their heads that were held up with dozens of clips, a hair net, and plenty of hairspray.

Brenda was engaged to Jim, a happy-go-lucky twenty-eight-year-old, who worked for a bakery as a salesman.

Hilary's fiancé, Gary, thirty-one, was a lorry driver who delivered garden sheds. Both were very kind to me. They both owned cars and never minded ferrying me anywhere around.

I spoke as I poured myself out a cup of tea. "How's life at that brassiere factory then girls?"

"Fine thanks," said Brenda. "How was your day at the nutty farm?"

Very good, I thought. *That's the way, give as good as you get.*

All three girls were employed within walking distance of home. Gloria worked behind the counter of the local post office. The two elder sisters worked together at a factory called Prestige Foundation Garments.

I slurped as I drank my tea. "Couldn't you get a job for our Gloria at that factory? She'd make a bloody good test pilot for your brassieres and corsets. If they'd fit her, they'd fit anybody!"

"I 'eard that, you nasty little sod!" shouted Gloria.

She wrestled to adjust her patent belt that was stretched tight around her middle. It was designed purely for decorative purposes, but trying to make her waist look smaller, she had fought to do it up three holes tighter than was comfortable. The effect was that the fat that belonged behind the belt divided itself above and below.

Mum started to dish out their meals. First a large mound of lumpy mash, followed by two slightly burnt sausages. I uncharacteristically picked at my meal and slowly my thoughts moved back to the events of this unusual day.

My mother spoke: "What's up with you then, son? Feeling a bit off colour? You're not constipated, are you?"

I snarled back at her. "God, Mother! That's your answer for almost everythin', innit? No, I'm not constipated actually. As a matter of fact I went at twenty past seven this mornin'."

"That's good then, my love," my mother purred back softly.

I carried on. "Not really. I didn't get out of bed 'til quarter past eight."

Gloria choked loudly on a mouthful of potato and the rest grinned.

As Mum picked up my plate and started to scrape the uneaten food into the pedal bin situated under the large enamel sink, she sighed. "What a bloody waste. There's millions in the world who'd love this."

"If you think I'm going to Africa with a plate of cold potato this time of night, you've got another thing coming," I joked.

Brenda interrupted before Mum could reply

to my levity. "Jim's got you some more records. I put 'em on your bed, Brian."

"Hooray!" I whooped and raced down the passageway and up the stairs two at a time.

For a couple of loaves of bread the landlord at Jim's local pub would give him all the old records off the jukebox. *Good old Jim!* I thought as I emptied the contents of the tatty carrier bag onto my blue bedspread. There were at least twenty and excitedly I sorted through them to see if I recognised any of the titles. I had hundreds of these records and although some of them were pretty scratched, I spent hours listening to them in my bedroom on my cream and red mono record player which was my last year's Christmas present.

I sat down on the bed and started to rummage through. *Dunno that one, dunno that one, don't know that one.* I stopped. What was this? I couldn't believe my luck! I'd always liked this particular record, but now, because of today, it meant so much more. *The Tears of a Clown*, I breathed. *The Tears of a Clown.*

My mind drifted back to my close encounter with Diane earlier and her voice echoed through my thoughts. "You really are a clown!"

I slowly stood up, holding the record like a new-born baby and meandered towards the record player. Gently, I placed it onto the turntable, flicked the start switch and with a clunk, the arm slumped onto the well-worn disc. I played the same record over and over and over, and as I did my mind slowly slid into a trance. Despair engulfed me as I savoured every word.

If there's a smile on my face, it's only there trying to fool the public

But when it comes down to fooling you, honey, that's quite a different subject

Although the words seemed to be tearing at my heart strings, I felt compelled to listen. The lyrics seemed to sum up my life story and inadequacies, and in a strange way it made me feel a real closeness to my new-found love.

As grief welled up inside me, I sobbed uncontrollably into my pillow.

After a thoughtful restless night, I got up. My head was pounding and my eyes were swollen from a night's morose weeping.

As I gazed into the bathroom mirror I decided that there would never be any future for my feelings, but I would at least try to make an effort.

I was not hygienically-minded, but this morning I scrubbed with Lifebuoy soap until my cheeks shone like rosy red apples. Then, I picked up the round tin with the red line that contained Gibbs toothpaste with its distinctive strange odour. I proceeded to scour my teeth until they bled.

Chapter 7: Floating Faggots

Mr & Mrs Moore lived with their wayward old English sheepdog at number forty, right next door to our house. They were both in their seventies and had lived in the same place over forty years. There was always plenty of friction between the two households, most of it caused by me. The frail little grey haired woman regularly took offence at my musical interludes and would knock on the wall. My mum would take offence at her pounding and would then reciprocate. Then Mrs Moore would knock back again. Many an evening the two women would sit either side of the wall playing Morse Code operators until the early hours.

Then, there was my football, which would always seem to find its way over the four foot high wall adjoining our two backyards. She would never just throw the ball back, but would always wait for me and my mother to knock on their front door and ask for it. It always ended in a verbal disagreement until eventually the cantankerous pensioner would hand the ball back over, stating that the next time it happened I wouldn't be getting it back.

Sometimes it was obvious by the large piles of doggy-doos in our back garden that the scraggy old mutt from next door was hurdling the wall, crapping, and then jumping back again into his own backyard. When this happened my inflamed mother would delight in picking up the excrement on a trowel and hurling it back over the wall, trying to hit their back door.

I spotted the slight figure of Mrs Moore approach as I waited impatiently for my overdue bus.

"Good morning, Brian," she uttered as she passed by.

"And a very good morning to you," I proclaimed sarcastically.

As she moved away and out of earshot I muttered, "You two-faced old cow!"

I fidgeted restlessly, shuffling from one foot to another. At last, when the bus came, I took a deep breath. I had quite forgotten how vigorously I had brushed my teeth earlier. "Shit!" I squealed as the icy air spiked into my head. "My teeth! They're bloody naked!"

The earth-shattering news came to me at my first lesson as I sat there with eyes peeled facing the classroom door, waiting apprehensively for the entrance of my dream girl.

Mr Thompson, the third-year head, spoke

as he entered. "If any of you are wondering where Diane Lewis is this morning, I will explain. Having assessed her capabilities yesterday, and contacted her previous schools, we have put her up to the next grade."

My heart sank as I slumped back into my seat. *Why is everything bloody against me?* I moaned.

The next few days fell into an inevitable void. I only caught a few glimpses of Diane in the playground at break or at lunch, but always she was surrounded by either the school Romeos or the mature, attractive girls, the sort that were completely out of bounds to a wimp like me. There was never an opportunity for me to speak to her and I doubted if I could bring myself to anyway. What was the point? The thoughts tortured me and the dull ache was still there in the pit of my stomach, but a sense of resignation deeply saddened me now.

My pride did me out of lunch the following week because as I marched into the hall to get my free dinner ticket, I caught sight of Diane queuing for her yellow ticket. Without hesitation I turned straight around and retreated, cursing all the while and wondering how I was going to get through the day without anything to eat.

I was ravenous when I arrived home that Monday evening and having called out the names of my family, I established that I was alone. A note on the kitchen table confirmed this:

Dear Brian,

Gone to get the shopping with Brenda and Jim.
Your dinner is in the stove.
Won't be long.

Love,
Mum

My empty tummy groaned loudly. I moved to the old stove. Hurriedly, I removed a covered plate from the oven. *Strange*, I thought as I lifted the lid and caught sight of dried up peas and chips in splendid isolation lying there. Times are getting hard. I threw the lid with the expert flick of the wrist into the washing up bowl in the sink and made my way towards the cupboard. Having completely smothered my meal in tomato ketchup, I wolfed it down so quickly that it seemed to lodge between my chest and my stomach. Then I decided to make myself a cup of tea to try and dislodge the lump. Just as I was about to drink it, in struggled the three weary shoppers laden with their grocery bags.

"All right my love?" panted Mum as she grappled to lift the heavy bags onto the table. "Did you 'ave your dinner?"

"Yes, ta, very nice. It could have done with a bit of meat on it though or summat."

"What are you on about?" Mum enquired as she waddled over to investigate. "There were two faggots on there."

"Oh no there wasn't – not when I got to it," I peeped.

My puzzled mother half-thought it was one of my jokes and waited for the punchline.

It was Brenda who found the solution as she turned on the tap to get herself a cup of water. She suddenly laughed out loud. "I can see what's happened, you silly little sod!" She chuckled, and they all moved nearer to observe.

Bobbing up and down in the dirty water were two faggots.

"They must have been stuck to the saucepan lid, you dafty swine! What a bloody waste!"

They all fell about laughing, including me, although later that evening I didn't think it was so funny as again my tummy started to rumble loudly.

Chapter 8: The School Trip

It seems strange to dress for school in jeans, sweatshirt and trainers, but the school trip was the one day it was possible to do so. Up until Diane Lewis coming on the scene I had been looking forward to the trip, but now it seemed of minor significance.

"Stay with the others, an' listen to the teachers," ordered Mother as she rammed egg sandwiches and crisps into my rucksack. "Watch the roads and do . . ."

I interrupted the lecture. "Mum, I'm going on a school trip outing, not off to soddin' war!"

Mum carried on. "I've 'eard about London. You're not too big to be murdered up an alley, or get run over by a tram."

I laughed. "Mother, I don't think they've still got trams in London, but I know what you mean."

My agitated mother brought her troubled expression to the front door. It was the one that was just a blink away from bursting into tears. She grabbed me roughly and kissed me on both cheeks. I wrestled away from her grip and hurried out.

"Be careful, my love! Be careful!" came

her distraught moan as I turned away.

She was still on the doorstep weeping and waving when I boarded the crowded bus. *I wouldn't be surprised if she stayed there all day*, I mused.

The shabby old coach was already there when I arrived at the school gates. I climbed the three steps onto the grotty-looking single-decker and realised that the rest of my class were already aboard. There were a few terse comments as I scanned the seating arrangements.

"We saved you a place, Bri!" shouted one of my so-called mates.

"Yeah, it's by your favourite bird!" blurted another.

Slowly it began to dawn on me what was going on. There were two empty seats behind the driver that were obviously reserved for the teachers. The only other vacancy was directly behind that right next to Josephine Smith, the class dog.

"You bleeders!" I muttered, as I realised I had been stitched right up.

The tickled onlookers all giggled as I grudgingly took my place.

Mr Perret, our history teacher, had organised this school trip to the National History

Museum. He always wore the same moth-eaten, scruffy clothes: a tweed jacket with leather elbow patches, corduroy trousers, and a knitted tie. His unruly mop of black hair stood up on end and horn rimmed glasses completed the look of a Mad Professor. He really looked a lot older than his thirty-eight years.

The best known secret in the school was the budding affair between him and the dark-haired games mistress, Miss Hartley. It was patently obvious to the rest of the staff and the pupils that this trip was just an elaborate plan by the adulterous Mr Perret to spend a few elicit hours with his lady love.

After a quick roll call the two lovebirds took their seats and the coach noisily shuddered into action. I shifted from one buttock to the other nervously, trying to edge myself as far away as I could from my enforced travelling companion without actually falling off the seat. I kept my gaze fixed firmly on the opposite window so as to avoid direct eye contact with this Creature from the Black Lagoon. The journey seemed endless as I fidgeted awkwardly, never once allowing myself to relax.

After about an hour, a soft voice broke the monotony. "What's the matter? Don't you like travelling on a coach?"

I begrudgingly turned to the direction of the question. "What makes you think that?" I whispered.

"Well, you don't seem to be enjoying yourself much."

As I squinted into Josephine's face a small part of me wanted to tell her exactly why I felt ill at ease, and what I felt about spending one of the most enjoyable days of the year perched next to the Bride of Frankenstein. But somehow I couldn't. Two weeks ago I would have. I just couldn't understand my change of attitude and my new compassionate nature.

She leaned towards me and smiled, revealing her large, uneven yellow teeth that were far too big for her lopsided mouth. As her lips peeled back over her tombstones, it revealed a saliva-covered brace on her top set. I found great difficulty in avoiding an expression of sheer revulsion, so I tried to lighten things up a bit.

"Ah, no, I'm always shy when I get near girls," I replied, batting my eyelashes hard in an expression of mock bashfulness.

Josephine laughed uncontrollably, sounding like a hyena with its nuts caught in a combine harvester. I cringed with embarrassment. I didn't want to be connected in any way with this outburst. *What a cute little laugh as well,*

I mused, as I nestled back into my seat, shut my eyes and pretended to doze.

As the coach drew to a halt, Mr Perret rose from his seat. "Right ladies and gentlemen, we have arrived. Now listen carefully. Miss Hartley and I have a few bits of business to take care of before we join you in the museum."

I bet you 'ave, you randy bleeder! I thought as I nodded to the teacher to signify that I had understood.

The teacher appeared not to notice as he continued with his instructions. "Therefore, I am relying on you all to conduct yourselves in an adult fashion. If by any chance our paths don't meet later, I want you all to be back on the coach prompt at 2:30 p.m. Any questions?"

"Yeah!" shouted a half-broken voice from the back seat. "Can we come outside the museum, Sir, to do a bit of sightseeing?"

"Definitely not!" barked back the teacher. "You must all stay within the confines of the building."

Everyone tutted.

Mr Perret added, "There's plenty to see, so don't moan, and remember, 2:30, prompt, back 'ere."

Chaos reigned momentarily as forty

adolescents pushed and barged, some trying to find their bags on the luggage rack and some trying to put on coats.

The two teachers made a guard of honour as the pupils jumped down. There was an occasional reminder about behaviour for the ones who were most at risk and then the two teachers disappeared back into the coach to obtain their belongings.

The large entrance hall was packed with tourists as the entire class spewed through the large wooden doors. A huge model of a dinosaur took pride of place right in the middle, with a skeleton of prehistoric birds swooping from the high ceiling either side.

Within a couple of minutes groups had been formed and all went different ways along various corridors. I stayed with Geoff Robinson and Steve Hawkham. Up one passageway and down another, occasionally stopping when something of interest caught our eye.

After forty-five minutes, however, we were bored to tears.

We came across a bench, so we sat and ate our pre-packed lunches, with the table manners of a couple of the exhibitors that we had just seen. As we finished we all stood up and proceeded to pack our debris back into our rucksacks. First the Tupperware containers, then the apple cores and silver paper.

Geoff suddenly stopped and looked up. "By the way, Bri, 'ow you getting on with that bit of skirt that I sorted out for you?"

"So it was you, you little git!" I howled as I took a swipe at Geoff's head, but he cleverly ducked and started to quicken his step away from me.

Steve then spoke up. "Yes, Brian, make sure she takes her braces off before you snog with her or you'll staple your lips together!"

Steve was already moving to avoid his light-hearted thump and was soon joined by his partner in crime as they both made off hastily.

I picked up my bag and raced after them. "I'll 'ave you, you pair of bleeders!" I shouted.

The chase was now well and truly on. They raced up stairways, along corridors, past displays of stuffed animals and Egyptian mummies, and then they came back into the entrance hall once again. I was hot on their heels. Bemused onlookers pressed themselves against the walls to avoid being bowled over as all three of us weaved our way through, all giggling with sheer devilment.

Just as Geoff and Steve reached a blind

corner, I decided I was near enough to make a dive for them. I caught the pair completely unawares as I lunged forward taking them both around their necks. All three of us lost our balance and with a helpless cry of "*shiiiiit!*", we all toppled with an almighty crash headlong through a display cabinet, landing amidst a shower of glass and broken wood into the arms of a huge stuffed gorilla, who looked menacingly down at us for disturbing his peace and quiet.

Breathlessly we gingerly disentangled ourselves from the wreckage and each other and then apologised profusely to the ape. We then cautiously stood up and brushed down the fragments from our clothes and hair, checking for injuries as we went. Miraculously we were all unscathed. The only thing being damaged at all seemed to be King Kong's pride.

We were all trying to straighten our dress when threading their way through the crowd came four large uniformed museum curators.

As they approached the one that could easily have been mistaken for a relation of Hitler bellowed, "What the hell d'you think you're playing at, you buggers!"

We all blushed and looked at each other frantically, hoping for an inspirational reply that just might lessen the consequences of this horrendous crime. After a deathly silence ensued, it was obvious that no such comment was forthcoming.

I feebly attempted to appeal to their better natures. I held my clenched fist towards them offering my wrists. "Put your cuffs on me mate, it was all my fault. It's a fair cop, but it really was an accident."

The inside of the large office was sparsely furnished, with just a large wooden desk next to an old tatty leather chair. There were four uncomfortable stools along the opposite wall. The smell of freshly painted walls filled the air.

"This stink makes me want to honk!" whispered Steve.

I nodded to him in agreement.

We all nervously shuffled our feet as the clock on the wall seemed to be noisily ticking our lives away.

We had been in the office since quarter to one. After a heated discussion between our four captors, the decision had been eventually reached that the best plan of action was to sit the delinquents in the office until 2:30 p.m. when they would be handed over to the teachers for punishment. It was an incredibly unnerving feeling watching the minutes tick ever near to another fateful confrontation. Our hearts began to beat faster as it reached the dreaded time, and when the tallest curator returned and glowered at us, we knew it was time. We were regimentally frogmarched out of the building towards the coach park.

The jungle drums had ensured that the rest of the class had already known what had happened and there was lots of noses pressed up against the coach windows as we arrived.

Mr Perret wore a puzzled frown as he saw the three of us, closely followed by the official looking museum officer.

"Are you the person in charge?" he exploded at the bemused teacher.

As he told his one-sided version of the story, Mr Perret's expression changed to one of flaming anger. The uniformed man gave them all a black look as he turned and strode away.

Mr Perret just stared at us and scoured, "Get in!"

We all sheepishly made our way onto the coach. Miss Hartley snorted disapprovingly as we passed and a restless silence descended on the whole class. The disgusted teachers stamped up the steps behind us and waited as we found our seats. He spoke, this time more calmly.

"It appears that a mindless few have let us and the good name of the school down and I take a very dim view to this. I will consider an appropriate punishment on the return journey."

He did a quick head count and then indicated to the driver that we could proceed.

Gradually normality came back and the laughing and joking started again. I just sat with my arms folded, staring into space, cursing my luck. In all the upheaval I hadn't thought of my Diane once. Now quietly sitting there, feeling rejected, I wondered about her and if she was all right. I wandered aimlessly through my dream world.

My seating companion spoke: "Tell me, Brian."

I turned to look straight into the eyes of Josephine Smith. *Corr, you're even uglier than I remembered*, I thought.

She spoke again. "If there's anything' I can do."

I tried to fight against my thoughts. All the compassion I had felt earlier for her had gone. I hardly dared to open my mouth for fear of what I might say to her, so I just glared at her.

My mind sifted through the punishment options that Mr Perret must be thinking of. It's possible we could get suspended, or even expelled. *Oh shit!* That would be awful. Our mum thinks the sun shines out of my arse.

My thoughts were interrupted by Mr Perret,

who was now leaning up on the seat looking around at everyone. "I've been thinking. Why should the actions of three thugs ruin the day for the rest of us? What say we have a sing song?"

An unenthusiastic "yeahhh" rang around the coach.

"Right, do anybody 'ave any requests?" He sensed the group's hostility, due to the impending sentence on the "Southleaze Three".

My sharp mind was working overtime as to how I could wangle a reprieve. I leant forward in my seat to gain the teacher's attention, then spoke discretely so that only Mr Perret could hear. "Sir, I know you're cross with me, but may I make a suggestion about what we might sing?"

In reply the teacher tutted and said, "Oh, go on then. What is it?"

"Well, Sir," I said confidently, "it's in the charts at the moment, but I can't remember the title."

"You're a bright one!" remarked Mr Perret.

"I know the words though, Sir," I went on. "You ought to listen . . . The first line is: I *hope my wife don't find out that I spent the day with my bit on the side*."

The defeated teacher gazed at me. He slowly turned and slid back into his seat. I relaxed back and heaved a sigh of relief. *Well that solves that one!* I smiled to myself.

Josephine leant over and whispered, "We can't sing that one Bri, I don't know the words."

Bloody hell! I thought. *Brains as well as looks!*

Chapter 9: It's a Dog's Life

"Hooray! He's home!" shrilled Hilary as she heard the front door slam behind me.

"I didn't know you cared," I sneered as I tramped into the kitchen grabbing a mangy-looking banana from the fruit bowl.

"It isn't that, I'm just glad you're back 'cos of our Mum."

"What's up then?" I enquired, slurping on a mouthful of the yellow fruit.

"What usually happens when she's worried?"

"Oh no! You don't mean . . ."

Hilary didn't let me finish. "Yes, you've guessed it. She has spent the day on the lavatory."

"Corr, bloody hell!" I cursed sourly.

"Language!" corrected Brenda as she appeared in the doorway.

"Well, it's enough to make anyone swear. You can't do anything without kick-starting her bowels into action. I'm just about sick of it!"

As I finished we all instinctively looked upwards towards the cobwebbed ceiling. The well-known "kerploosh" resounded as the medieval flush was pulled. We waited in anticipation as the footsteps drew closer.

After a tearful reunion, and a censored version of the day's events, we all sat down and tucked into our large dishes of pork bone stew.

"I'll say this for you though, Mum. You may be a pain in the arse, but you're the best cook in the world!" I said enthusiastically. I stabbed a large steaming doughboy from my dish and then gnawed on it like a toffee apple.

"Shut your gob and eat!" howled Mum.

After the dishes had been cleared away, Gloria returned from her usual Wednesday night overtime. Then we all drifted one-by-one into the back room to watch the news.

As Mother bent over the top of the television to put the wall plug in, she spoke: "That's what I meant to say to you, Bri. I found a note in your blazer, something about a careers evening tomorrow night?"

"What the 'ell was you doing looking in my pockets?" I yelled as I sat up straight from my hand-warming position by the heater.

"Oh, um, I didn't mean to look, love, I sort of . . . I just couldn't help it."

"I'll put a soddin' mousetrap in there one day!" I retorted, cupping my hands once more over the burning red element.

"Well what about it, son?" she went on,

wiggling into her seat on the sofa between Gloria and Hilary.

"Yes, there is a meeting and yes, I would like to go, but it doesn't start until seven o'clock and it's dark then, remember?" I spouted sarcastically.

Hilary piped up, "Well, I think he ought to go. It's important for his future."

Mother put excuse after excuse why I shouldn't go: I had a weak chest and I couldn't go out at night, oh and it was her bingo night as well with Aunty Hilda. Each weak argument was quickly flaunted by the girls, who all felt strongly that I should be allowed to go.

When all the arguments were finished it had been decided that Jim would drop me up the school on his way to darts. There would be lots of boys coming home together on the bus and I could do the same, provided that I promised to stay with the group.

We all settled back to an evening's viewing and Mother very soon assumed her usual pose – eyes closed, mouth open, snoring loudly.

It was about half past eight when the peace and tranquillity was brought to an abrupt conclusion with the sound of a sharp knock at the front door.

Mum   sprang   forward   returning   to

consciousness. "Who is it?!" she yelled. This was one of her most annoying habits, as every time she heard the knock at the front door, she seemed to think that everyone else was capable of seeing through walls to see who was visiting.

This time there wasn't an opportunity for any of us to respond to our mother as the urgency of the knock seemed to stun us all into silence. Instinctively we fought to make our way hastily to the front door. Brenda was the first there and before the door could be fully opened, the sound of a high-pitched whine rang out.

It was Mrs Moore from next door, looking as frail as ever. She struggled to catch her breath as she fought through the tears to speak. "It's . . . it's George!" she wailed, pointing over Mother's shoulder.

"What about George?" screamed our mum.

"He's in your garden and he's hurt!"

"He's what?" questioned Gloria as we all jockeyed for position in the overcrowded hallway.

The fraught Mrs Moore went on: "We must hurry, he could be dying!"

The whole Wilson family, like characters in a Keystone Cops movie, scrambled in one lump along the passageway, through the kitchen, and out of the back door and into the yard. To our shock and horror we found a distressed Mr Moore lying on his back with his legs in the air, just like a beetle who had been overturned and was unable to right himself.

"Be careful with 'im!" shouted Mother as we all clambered towards him.

Mrs Moore shuffled her way through and knelt down beside him. "George, my love! Are you all right?" she wailed, cradling his head gently from the cold hard concrete.

His eyes flickered and then opened. With a painful moan he whimpered, "I think I'm all right, help me up."

Everyone surrounded the prostrate senior citizen and very gingerly raised him to a tottering stance. Mum held open the back door. Hilary grabbed one arm and Mrs Moore the other as they slowly guided the shaken old boy into the house.

"Sit 'im down. I'll make him a nice strong cup of tea," commanded Mum.

The two bearers eased the frail old gent into a chair and then both sat either side of him. It took half an hour, and three cups of tea, before the shocked pensioner was together enough to relate his sorry tale of how he came to find himself in such a predicament. Apparently, he had gone into the garden to look for his unruly dog, and had found that the large mutt had been just about to do his business in our garden. He had climbed onto the wall to try to coax the disobedient dog back over, but lost his balance and just like Humpty Dumpty, he had fallen off of the wall. The exasperating canine was back in his basket before Mrs Moore had even discovered that her husband was missing.

As they talked together their old differences were forgotten as Mum and Mrs Moore spoke civilly to each other for the first time in years.

Arm in arm, the old couple left our household to return to their own dwelling.

All the old grievances would have been forgotten forever if Mother could have only controlled her tongue for just one more minute, for as she escorted her elderly neighbours along the pavement, she declared loudly, "Oh by the way, Mrs Moore . . ."

"Yes, my love?" answered the old lady softly.

Then she let her have it, my favourite remark of all time: "If he comes over the wall again, you aren't bloody having him back!"

Chapter 10: Love Hurts

Most large state-run schools have a lawless element and Southleaze was no exception.

As I thanked Jim and slammed shut the door of his dark brown Hillman Minx, the two most notorious hoodlums screamed past on their Lambretta motor scooters. Dean Hardy and Adrian Kuzeki were both sixteen and instilled fear and trepidation into both pupils and teachers alike. The Hardy and Kuzeki families were notorious for their complete disregard for anyone and anything. They operated a Mafia-style protection racket within the area. It was commonplace to see police at the school investigating something sinister concerning their illegal activities. Everything about them was purposely controversial. Their radical appearance enhanced them as cult figures amongst the impressionable youngsters of the school.

When the skinhead look became popular, the two were not content to have their hair cut short – it had to be completely shaved off, which resulted in them looking meaner and more threatening than ever. Their clothes were also way over the top. Their jeans were so short that it looked like they had had a row with their ankles and their Dr Martens bovver boots were painstakingly buffed to a mirror finish.

As with all good Mods, their pride and joy was their motor scooters. Each gleaming machine was customised with chrome sides and a high fur-backed headrest. The fronts were decorated with a mass of spotlights and mirrors. As they hurtled past I muttered, *I wonder if they bleeders know that I 'ave a scooter!* Trouble is, it's made by Triang and I have to scoot along with one foot.

I tapped twice on the roof of the car and it lumbered away and into the night. There was a strange transparent orange aura silhouetting the buildings as the bright lights of the school met with the cold foggy evening.

I mingled with the pupils and parents, who were arriving and making their way to the main entrance and into the school hall.

As I glanced about, taking in all around me, I was pleasantly surprised at the lavish preparation that had gone on for this event. I imagined that it would take the form of a lecture on various job opportunities, but no, this was far more interesting. It almost had the appearance of the autumn fair. Most of the school floor area was covered with many colourful, brightly-lit stands. Every display had a particular career theme, with many photographs and leaflets on each occupation. Members of staff were milling about and if you showed interest, would take the time to inform you more about what positions were available and what qualifications were necessary.

There didn't seem to be any of my close friends about, but I still enjoyed the atmosphere and talked to many teachers with a new-found serious, mature attitude.

The clatter of a metal roll-up shutter made everyone's head turn. As it was raised it revealed two female teachers pouring hot drinks from a huge teapot into rows of plastic cups.

Mr Longton made his way cautiously up the five steps at the side of the stage. Having reached the top, he clapped his hands three times to attract everyone's attention. As he spoke he pointed in the direction of the kitchens. "Ladies and gentlemen, thank you all very much for attended this evening and making this venture such a success. Refreshments are now being served." He half bowed and then descended to retake his place amongst the multitude.

As people were slowly edging towards the free drinks, a gap appeared in the crowd and there she was, standing alone, Diane. Instantly she was the only person in the room. My ears became sealed to all the sounds, other than the loud rhythmic pounding of my heartbeat. As I stared she gave a little wave and started to walk towards me. A little voice inside my head started nagging, *Don't get the wrong idea, Brian, she's not interested in you mate. It's just that you're the only one here that she knows. Pull yourself together, you know she's out of your league.* My heart was pounding so hard I felt that she would surely hear it, but I couldn't help ignoring my inner warnings.

The elegant girl smiled cutely and spoke. "Hi Brian, I'm really glad to see you. I was beginning to think that I was the only third year who had made the effort."

I told you so. My heart sank as my inner voice rubbed salt into the wound.

My face must have portrayed my disappointment as quickly Diane spoke again: "Oh I'm sorry, Brian! I didn't mean you were, um, you know, um, that I'm only glad because, you know, um . . ."

She became more and more tongue-tied and frustrated as she stammered to correct her faux pas.

On recognising this I gallantly used a few well-chosen words. "Can I get you a coffee?" I was so very pleased with my confident response, and so was Diane because she stopped trying to negotiate an apology and rested the flat of her hand across her neck.

She sighed with relief, then gratefully explained, "Thank you, Brian, that would be lovely."

As I smugly strode away, I turned and announced, "Stay there, Diane, I won't be long." I kicked my heels whilst I was waiting to be served, doing it hard enough at one point actually to dent my right ankle just to prove to myself that I was awake and that this was not a dream. I couldn't believe how I had coped with the last situation. *I must be sickening or summat*, I mused. *That wasn't how the prize prick I've grown to know and love would normally have handled that situation.*

The chance of a free hot drink was turning the once orderly crowd into an unruly mob of pushers and shovers. More and more moved to join the rugby scrum forming around the serving hatch. Eventually I sneaked through a small gap between two fat women and grabbed two coffees. I thought it had been difficult enough getting there, but trying to back out through the chaos, balancing two wobbly plastic cups, was proving impossible.

After much barging, and ninety-four excuse me's, I freed myself from the thoughtless herd of people. Eyes firmly fixed on the coffee, I concentrated hard keeping them level, walking rigidly like a new form of the egg and spoon race. I was becoming increasingly aware of the heat on my fingertips. I knew that I had only a few seconds before the drinks would become too hot to handle. *Quick, quick, quick!* I howled as I bumped past two figures. I hastily delivered the two steaming receptacles into Diane's outstretched hands. As I sucked on my scorched fingers, I sensed an uneasiness in Diane's manner. Glancing around I understood why, for not four feet away from us were the villainous duo that I had seen outside earlier. My eyes sprang open wide and blood drained from my face as absolute horror engulfed me.

The swarthy skinhead Kuzeki snarled menacingly at me. "Who d'you think you're pushing, you little bastard?"

Diane quickly defended me. "He didn't mean to, he was just burning himself."

The other poker faced reprobate snorted in a deep voice, "Shut your face, blondie, or we'll rearrange it!"

This brought a surge of uncommon courage to shrug off my fear. I blurted back at them, "Don't speak to her like that or I'll . . ."

"You'll what?" ridiculed the surprised Dean Hardy.

It had thrown the aggressive pair completely off guard to have someone stand up to them, so they just stood glowering at each other, lost for words. Kuzeki nodded his head towards the main door. They turned and walked out without looking back.

My uncommon bravery was now dwindling fast and replacing the incensed anger was a sickly feeling at the back of my throat and an uncontrollable tremble. My two shaking hands precariously tried to hold onto my coffee cup.

"Are you all right Brian?" enquired Diane, placing her hand on my shoulders.

I couldn't control the quiver in my voice. "Yeah, ta, they don't frighten me!"

Diane's entire face radiated as she gazed fondly at her Sir Galahad. As she finished her drink she asked, "Did your mum and dad come with you tonight, Brian?"

"Err, no, they couldn't make it. Did yours?"

"Yes, there are my old folks over there, talking to Miss Hartley," she replied.

My curiosity to know everything about her made me spin quickly around to observe the couple who were responsible for this beautiful creation. As my eyes zoomed in, my mood again slumped. *Oh shit!* I might have bloody guessed it. I was hoping in some way that Diane's parents might have been the chink in her immaculate armour. Far from it. Mr Lewis was a good-looking, thirty-seven-year-old, with jet black, tightly curled hair. He looked every inch the successful businessman as he confidently pushed his hands into the trouser pockets of his impeccable navy blue pinstripe suit. I bit on my lip as my gaze moved to Mrs Lewis.

The sight of this beautiful woman nearly made me scream with anguish as I feasted my eyes on the fully-developed version of the girl next to me. *Why can't they be bloody old or ugly?* I pondered. I saw the flawless pair as two more bricks in the increasingly impenetrable wall between myself and my female pipe dream.

"If you want I'll get my dad to give you a lift home," offered Diane.

You got to be sodding joking, I thought. *I don't want you lot knowing where I live.* I began to panic as I conjured up an excuse. "No thanks. I got a lift home. Ooh is that the time? I got to be going."

I frantically said my goodbyes as I backed away, just like Cinderella leaving the ball at midnight.

The weather outside had deteriorated dramatically and now a thick blanket of freezing fog masked the familiar surroundings. I stood nervously in the school entrance trying to compose myself before my inevitable dive into the bleak night. With one last deep breath I swung the large glass door back and scurried out into the murky night.

Landseer Square was only four hundred yards from Southleaze School, but in this pea souper it became four miles. Within seconds of leaving the sanctuary of the warm comfortable school, I was fumbling blindly along the usually busy Sheldon Street, without even a car light to break the eerie shroud that engulfed me. I trotted cautiously along, arms out in front, like a sleepwalker trying to avoid stumbling into something. The backs of my legs began to tighten and ache as I desperately blundered along, ever closer to the refuge of my public transport.

Through the ghostly cloud I eventually caught sight of the distant illuminations of the parked bus at the terminus. I breathed a heavy sigh of relief. *Thank Christ for that!* I gasped, allowing myself to slow my pace and relax a little. I was only thirty yards from the safety of the number twenty-two bus when the violent attack took place.

From nowhere a hard punch to the side of my face sent me reeling. Confusion and pain ran through my head as another fist hammered into my stomach. As I hunched myself over for protection against any more pounding, a sickening crunch blinded me as an upward thrusting boot broke my nose. All resistance had now drained from my body. A numbness now replaced the violated areas of excruciating pain. My legs buckled and I crumpled helplessly to the ground, my face bouncing on the cold rough pavement.

Before making off as swiftly as they had pounced, the cowardly attackers reigned a torrent of merciless kicks to my lifeless head and body. As I lay motionless, warm tears mixed with the blood from my torn face and ran down into a puddle beneath my head. I now drifted into a swirling, uneasy dream world and out of suffering.

Chapter 11: Long Road to Recovery

It wasn't a sudden and complete return to awareness, but a fretful and painful rough ride slowly back into semi-consciousness. Faintly in the distance I could hear my name being whispered and the unmistakable wail of my mother's crying. My injured body was unable and unwilling to respond to this hint of life, so I lapsed once again back into a restless sleep.

When I finally roused myself, the bright glare of the fluorescent lights above me stung my battered and bruised eyes. I fought to take in air through my swollen lips. My misshapen nose was completely blocked with congealed blood. My confused aching head was now trying to comprehend the situation. Flashes of the previous night's beating started flickering through my befuddled mind. At the time everything had happened so fast, I'd not had time to be frightened, but now as the nightmare started to unfold before me, my whole body began to shake violently as I became more and more distressed. Tears of disbelief started to flow.

A petite student nurse, who was sat at the

desk in the corner, noticed my stirring and hurried towards me. She whispered sweetly as she came alongside my quivering body, "Hello poppet, what's the matter?"

With great difficulty and pain I turned my stiff neck towards the concerned blue-uniformed nurse. She noticed with sympathy my grief-stricken face and patted my forearm softly. "Shh, shh, there, there, it's all over Brian, and you're going to be all right."

After more comforting words she picked up a water-filled tumbler and a drinking straw from the bedside cabinet. Then she offered me a drink.

In response I managed to croak a weak, "Yes please".

She placed her right hand beneath my head and gently lifted it slowly from the starched white pillow. She held the glass close to my chin and placed the straw between my pursed lips. I slurped loudly and then gagged as I tried to negotiate drinking and breathing at the same time. She only allowed me a few sips before slowly lowering my head back down into the previous position resting on the pillow.

"There, I bet you feel better already," she said, smiling broadly at me.

It had calmed me down slightly and I did feel less threatened.

The nineteen-year-old trainee nurse spoke again: "Your mother and sisters have only just left to get something to eat. They should be back soon. What a surprise they will have when they see you back in the land of the living!"

She lifted the sleeve of my hospital issue smock and wrapped a green cloth band around the top of my arm, securing it with a tie. She then put a stethoscope to her ear and held the other end to my upper arm. She pumped at a small black rubber ball attached to it. The band grew tighter and tighter. She watched intently, a bead of mercury rising on the blood pressure meter. I grimaced as the cuff grew unbearably tight and then the nurse released the pressure valve and the fluid immediately dropped and the band deflated and it stopped hurting.

"You'll have to get used to that. We have to do that every half hour for the next twenty-four hours. It's all part of having you under observation."

As carefully as she could she took my temperature, checked my pulse and shone a glaring little torch into my eyes. As she stood noting her findings onto the chart taken from the foot of my bed, a tall fresh-faced doctor appeared and asked how I was feeling. The well-spoken intern explained that although the injuries that I had sustained were only superficial, I was being kept in for a few days, just to be on the safe side.

Superficial? I thought, gradually regaining my marbles. *I feel like I've been run over by a bloody steamroller!*

Both my attendants said goodbye and walked through the swing doors and out of the ward.

Mother was informed of my recovery as she and my three sisters returned from the cafeteria. After a desperately anxious all-night vigil by my bed, the news of my return from oblivion was greeted with whoops of joy and a skip in their overwrought steps as they eagerly made their way back to ward twenty-three.

The bedraggled Wilson quartet made their usual flamboyant entrance, almost knocking over a short plump Jamaican auxiliary as she served a mid-morning cup of tea to an elderly patient. She mumbled a few ethnic obscenities and tutted, before leaning her formidable frame into her creaky old trolley and pushing it towards the next bed.

Mother grabbed my hand and held it to her blotchy red cheek. From her handbag she produced a saturated length of white toilet roll and proceeded to add more tears to it. She gazed into my puffy black eyes and sobbed.

"Thank God you're all right! We were so worried."

For the first time in years I felt frail and very despondent. I never had imagined that I would see the day when I would need my oddball family around me as I did now. I choked on a lump forming in my raw throat and then wept uncontrollably. My three distressed sisters stood solemnly in a line on the other side of the bed. They each instinctively grabbed a part of my disfigured body and joined Mum and me in a resounding mass cry.

The whole ward came to a standstill and ogled at the noisy scene.

A ginger-haired staff nurse, who was busy adjusting one of the wee brigade's catheters, heard the uproar and left her duties and moved rapidly to the unhappy throng. She majestically whisked the tatty flowered curtain around the weeping family to give us privacy at this emotional time.

After a lot of painful hugs and slobbery kisses the mood began to ease. My whole family sniffed continually and wiped their tired eyes. I didn't because it felt like I had two red hot pokers preventing my nostrils from performing their designated functions.

Brenda coughed loudly into her hankie and said inquisitively, "What happened, Bri?

Who'd do such a terrible thing to you?"

All the females waited with baited breath for details of the savage ambush.

I lifted my heavy arm that lay beside me and noticed that I had grazes along my knuckles. I scratched my forehead. My scrambled brain struggled to provide an answer and although confusion still shrouded much of the previous evening's events, strong tormented feelings tore at me and I felt I needed much more time and soul searching before being willing to commit myself to any statement. I even wanted to keep the identity of the mindless beasts responsible to myself. Not to protect them, but even at this early stage, only a few hours after the incident, considered myself to be very lucky, for knowing Kuzeki and Hardy's past record getting away without even a broken arm or leg was something of a minor miracle.

I was also very concerned for Diane's safety. If this beating up could be the end of the matter for both of us, that would be peace of mind enough. What would be the point anyway? I knew that the two villains were way above the law and would eventually catch up with anyone who split on them. That would surely mean permanent rearrangement of my features.

A cold shiver ran down my spine and in a

squeaky voice I replied, "I dunno. They come up from behind."

Hilary sensed uneasiness in my reaction and spurred me on with a grin. "Come on! You know who it was. Why don't you tell us?"

"They crept up on me," I insisted. "I ain't got a clue who they were, now leave me alone!"

I placed the back of my hand across my eyes to protect them from the searing light and to signify to my inquisitors that I didn't want to speak anymore. My head began to thump in time to my accelerated heartbeat and I was becoming very fidgety and agitated.

"All right, son, all right, don't fret," reassured my mum, running her chubby wrinkled fingers through my uncombed greasy hair. "Plenty of time for questions. We're just glad to see that you're on the mend." She shot a look to Hilary and the eldest daughter reluctantly put things right by excusing her last comments.

"Yes, Brian, I'm sorry. I didn't mean to disbelieve you. Just get well, eh love?"

I nodded from behind my blood-spattered hand and closed my aching eyes.

Gloria spoke softly. "Come on, we ought to let 'im rest now. We can go home happy knowing that he's gonna be all right."

They nodded to one another and then in turn kissed me before leaving me in peace.

On the way out Mother complained bitterly to a middle-aged woman at reception about me being in the ward where I was the youngest by about fifty years. The apologetic excuse given was that unfortunately, there was an acute bed shortage in this outdated Victorian establishment and the short stay observation cases simply had to be put anywhere that there was a vacant space and adequate nursing cover.

After the initial shock and realisation of my injuries, I began to cope well with my aches and pains and although I would never let on to anyone else, I started to enjoy the deviation from my normal humdrum existence. I wallowed in the sympathy of the nurses and found the walking wounded of the ward very entertaining, as one by one they would sit on the end of my bed and introduce themselves before divulging their secrets of their case histories. I was fascinated by the stories of their various ailments and diseases.

One sprightly grey haired seventy-year-old even insisted on graphically describing, with the aid of detailed drawings that were illuminated with different coloured crayons, the downfall of his bowels and bladder over the last thirty years. He even demanded that he show me where they fitted the catheter, lifting up his nightshirt to reveal a dangling hosepipe attached with a plaster to the end of his shrivelled manhood.

The clatter of the food trolley could be heard unceremoniously being shoved through the doors. It was crammed full with various sized metal containers. Lumbering along behind, clumsily pushing, was the disinterested ebony-skinned auxiliary. She manoeuvred it into the middle of the floor and then noisily applied the brake which was part of one of the front wheels. Three young nurses came scurrying from different directions to help serve up.

As one nurse passed, she cheerfully asked, "D'you think you could manage a bit of lunch my love?"

I lifted my head, half glanced at the old man still perched on the end of my bed like a garden gnome, and croaked, "Yeah I suppose so, as long as it isn't chipolatas."

Chapter 12: Police! Police!

The meticulous hospital routine and lengthy visiting times, when the Wilson clan would converge bearing armfuls of get well gifts, didn't seem to leave much time for serious thinking. So I decided to forget my impossible struggles in the world outside and allow myself to be carried along on a wave of comforting words and kind actions from all and sundry. It felt as if I was on a much needed holiday.

The only uneasy moments occurred on the third day. I was relaxing on top of the bed clothes, scanning a football magazine and munching on a large wedge of homemade bread pudding that my mum had brought in the previous evening, when two uniformed policemen in their early thirties descended on me. I heard the sound of approaching flat feet and looked up to find the pair of them removing their tit-shaped helmets and placing them strategically onto my bed. I felt a bit nervy, but I'd been half expecting an interrogation of some kind, so I had a well-rehearsed, unhelpful, nondescript statement already prepared for this situation.

The nearer of the two law enforcers had sparkling ice-blue eyes and neat, short, cropped black hair that most girls would have given their eyeteeth for. A long pointed nose and a protruding dimpled chin ruined his natural attributes, making him look like the result of the card game that I possessed. In it you build up funny faces with different unsuitable features. He undid the button on his tunic pocket and produced a small red notepad. He dabbed the end of the pencil on his outstretched tongue, then attempted to sound official by overemphasizing the first letter of every word.

"Ello Brian, we would like you, in your own words, to tell us what happened on the evening when you were attacked."

I quickly decided that it sounded more credible if I acted a little simple, so I replied in an empty emotionless manner, "Dunno really. I can't remember."

The other Latin-looking officer ran a hand uneasily through his swept back, Brylcreamed hair and gave a bemused frown. It didn't surprise me that when he spoke his accent bore a distinct resemblance to that of an Italian restaurant owner.

"Are-you-a sure-a?" he questioned.

I rapidly replied, "Yes-a – I'm-a sure-a."

I feared that my quick-fire impersonation may have fallen on sticky ground, so I hastily adopted my unintelligent attitude again. I hoped that they hadn't heard. "Yes, I'm sure, it all happened so fast," I drooled.

"You didn't hear or see any motor scooters, did you?" said the first officer in his testifying-in-court voice.

"No I never," I lied. "I didn't see nothin'. Corr my head 'urts."

"All right son, just a few more questions," said the disconcerted constable, hoping to be able to write something juicy into his empty pad.

After a bit more cross-examination they both decided that any more quizzing would be useless, so they reluctantly wished me well and asked me that if I did remember anything of significance, that I would contact them immediately.

Proudly gowning themselves once again in their regulation head gear, they nodded to the ward sister as they marched out.

Just after lunch on that Tuesday afternoon, I was informed by a softly-spoken staff nurse that Mr Parker, the consultant, would probably allow me home tomorrow after I had been examined. I felt quite ashamed with myself for not being overjoyed at the news, but instead I tried to hide the disappointment that I felt inside. I didn't really want to leave this warm insular cocoon. To brave the harsh reality of the real world again. To think for myself, and to face more of life's traumas.

Chapter 13: Dishing Out the Chores

Mother was ecstatic when she heard the news of my pending homecoming as she visited me on the Tuesday evening. She sent Jim straight home to fetch my holdall full of clean clothes for her baby to wear the following morning on my homeward journey.

All the family had hated not having me around with my effervescent nature, but would all rather miss their daily excursions to the hospital. This was a temporary escape from their dull, predictable existence. Mum hadn't been out of the house so much in years and it had given her a good opportunity to christen three new gaudy dresses that had been hanging in her mahogany wardrobe for at least the last decade.

The girls spent hours painstakingly dolling themselves up and styling their hair, especially Gloria who lavishly caked on her makeup and tried to make herself look as attractive as possible. Unfortunately, it had had the reverse effect, only making her look like a third rate drag queen on a bad day. She would childishly fantasize that her looks may impress a handsome unattached young doctor and plunge her into an adventure of a steamy romance. The plan had failed miserably, not even the oversexed geriatric patients of ward twenty-three, who had been without female company for a long time, had given her a second glance, except to wonder whether it was a male or a female.

As they arrived back home on that Tuesday night, Mum demanded that they all should sit in the front room, where she would designate various tasks to each family member.

"Right, you lot, you all have to take tomorrow off. I want it to be just right for when my little lamb comes home."

Gary, not daring to cross her, stood motionless, studying the threadbare carpet as the list of chores was eloquently rattled off.

"Right, young man, we can use your car to fetch Brian, and of course I'm coming with you."

"Hang on, Mum," interrupted Brenda. "Aren't you jumping the gun a little bit? We don't even know if he's coming home for sure."

Mother didn't need to utter a reply. Her stony glare snaked around the room until it found its target, making Brenda freeze in mid-flight.

"Sorry, sorry!" said Brenda apologetically, raising both hands in a gesture of defeat.

"As I was saying," continued Mum, "we'll use Gary's car, cos it's better looking than Jim's."

"Sorry I'm sure!" said Jim sarcastically.

Brenda knew better than to incur Mum's wrath when it was in full flow, so she elbowed Jim in the side.

"Jim? Don't think you're getting away with it. You're going to come over here tomorrow and help our Brenda with the shopping. We'll need to get a good few things in that's Brian's favourites, and if you're very lucky, my lad, I'll even let you pay for the little treats."

"Thank you very much," muttered Jim, knowing full well that there was absolutely no point in retaliating when Mother was in this forceful mood.

Hilary and Gloria looked at each other and grinned like Cheshire cats at the sight of Jim being brought to heel by their steamed-up mother.

"I don't know what you two are looking so smug about. You aint heard what your bit is yet!" she blasted.

The two girls swivelled their heads around to the direction of their mother.

"I want this house cleaned from top to bottom so it's gleaming like a pin. That's your job."

Their grins dropped immediately from their

faces and Hilary dared to comment. "Mum, don't mind me asking, but what are you gonna be doing when all this is going on?"

Mum's expression instantly changed to her little-girl-lost look and a tear glistened in the corner of her left eye. She spoke, this time in a frail, broken voice: "That's right, make your old mum feel rotten. I'm just excited about having my baby back home."

They all stared at each other and smirked, recognising that their astonishing manipulative mother had just got them all over an emotional barrel once again. You could see where I got it from.

Chapter 14: The Get-Well Symphony

The lights on the ward were lowered to a subdued level and all the patients were settling themselves down for a long night ahead. I felt wide awake, without a hint of tiredness, physically or mentally. I dreaded the upheaval and the change that tomorrow morning would bring. I tried to draw my thinking away from negative thoughts, but it was no good. A cold, clammy sweat began to weld my itchy pyjamas to my back. I punched and prodded my rock-hard pillows several times, hoping that it might magically help, but nothing did.

On nights before I had fallen asleep before lights out, but tonight there was no chance of that. I watched as the shadowy figure of a nurse scampered past carrying a bed pan covered with a cloth. I heard the muted moan of an ailing eighty-five-year-old three beds up, and then it started. Something I knew nothing about. It was the ward twenty-three all-male orchestra.

Tonight's performance kicked off with old Bill Hawkins in the next bed. Firstly, he let out a throaty snore which lasted about five seconds, and then a long high-pitched whistle through his open mouth. I had never heard anything like it. I stared at the horizontal figure alongside me, moving rhythmically up and down as he slept. Then, as I watched, the rasping sound of a pyjama-splitting fart rang out from the far end of the ward. This seemed to be the signal for all of the wind section to commence. Within seconds a bizarre overture was being performed up and down the length of the beds opposite. Those who weren't breaking wind either coughed, sighed or snored.

Before very long everyone except me had joined in, in one way or another.

As I observed I soon began to appreciate the humour in this unique spectacle. I began to giggle uncontrollably. I stuffed a clenched fist into my mouth to stifle my laughter. I pulled the sheets high over my head to block out my surroundings. The change of mood made me quite forget about going home and before long sleep had crept over me.

Chapter 15: House Proud

Being only used to loose pyjamas for over a week, now fully clothed, I began to feel incredibly claustrophobic. I pulled at the neck of my navy-blue pullover, trying to stretch it and make it more comfortable. I wandered aimlessly around, now resigned to my impending freedom.

I entered one last time through the open door of the ward's bathroom. I examined myself closely in the polished mirror above the large white wash basin. I still sported a sore-looking scab on my nose, but the swelling about my eyes and mouth seemed to have receded. The bruises that were a painful black and blue a few days ago had now lightened to a delicate tone of yellow and brown. I ran my fingers across my stomach to assess the healing of my damaged ribs. There were still some quite tender areas. I grimaced as my inquisitive touch came into contact with sensitive spots.

I emerged into the ward again just as the grey-haired consultant who had pronounced me fit moments earlier stomped past. He didn't look one way or the other, with his hands firmly clenched behind his back. An entourage of male and female junior doctors hurried to keep up with him as he made his way onto the next ward on his busy agenda. I took a hasty step backwards to avoid being trampled on in the rush and then sauntered back to my bed.

I started to flick aimlessly through the pile of magazines, glancing at the big round clock. I noticed it was ten past ten. *Another twenty minutes*, I thought, and it was back to reality. *Oh shit!*

42 Gilbertson Street was a hive of frenzied activity from the crack of dawn. The hyped-up Joyce Wilson leapt from her bed to switch off her old-fashioned alarm clock two hours before it was due to wake her. Her excitement and nervous energy hadn't allowed her more than a light doze all night. Her tacky dry mouth made her long for her first morning cuppa. She noisily dressed, bumping around the bedroom, ensuring that her daughters were not to have much more rest on this important day.

The girls appeared one by one into the cold, dank kitchen, all looking like something the cat had dragged in. Their hair bore resemblance of hurricane damage. Their eyes were heavily smeared with the remainder of yesterday's dark makeup, giving them all the appearance of giant pandas. They staggered in precariously wrapped in their gaudy pink shiny dressing gowns, bodies feeling quite numb from being prematurely plucked from their much-needed beauty sleep.

"What the hell's the time, Mum?" drooled Hilary, trying to persuade her falling beehive to sit back on top of her head, rather than droop like a dead rat over her left ear.

Mum looked hard at her chubby wrist and answered loudly, "It's nearly half past six and there's a lot to be done."

Gloria slumped limply onto one of the wooden kitchen chairs, her bare thighs slapping together as they hit the icy cold seat. She clumsily put her elbows onto the table in front of her and plunged her head deep into her upturned hands. "Oh Christ!" she moaned. "Is that all the time is? We all must be bloody mad! It's the middle of the night."

Mum barked back, "Don't be stupid!" She playfully flipped her daughter around the head.

Brenda made her way, more out of reflex than desire, to the ancient gas stove. She lifted the battered kettle, then with eyes still half-closed moved unsteadily towards the constantly dripping tap.

Mum sprang to her feet and easily took the kettle from her weak grip. "Sit down, lovely, I'll do that," she said warmly, pushing the youngest daughter into the seat next to Gloria. Mrs Crafty Wilson knew that the day was far too young to have it ruined by a mutiny from her daughters. She knew she relied on their help and the efforts of their men friends to make this day go smoothly, so she decided to try to be nice, making amends for the harshness of her manner the night before when she had press-ganged them into their involvement.

They could see through the unusual early morning kindness, but were all far too knackered to object to having someone wait on them. Even in this fatigued state, they all realised that this was just a fleeting glimpse of the calm that would quickly be changed to the raging storm.

They were all totally right. By a quarter to eight she had them all running around the house at breakneck speed, not knowing whether they were on their arses or their elbows. For one split second though Gloria did, for as she scurried down a passageway, unaware that Hilary had just vigorously polished the lino beneath, a strip of carpet shot out from underneath her, sending her sprawling ungainly like a dying swan. She definitely knew painfully that she was on her arse.

Just as Mother and her workforce had

downed dusters for a well-earned brew, Jim arrived, prepared for his enforced spending spree. As he entered he pinched his nose with thumb and forefinger and exclaimed, "Poo, what a pong!"

Mum shouted back, "It's only Pledge. Don't your lazy mother ever use it?"

Jim refused to be drawn in by the woman's instinctive sarcasm, just biting lightly into his bottom lip. "Ungrateful old cow!" he thought. "I'm losing a day's pay and getting collared into buying presents for her precious son."

Brenda sensed Jim's growing anger and fumbled to catch hold of his hand. She squeezed, a wink and a smile from her was enough to calm him sufficiently to join her and her sisters around the spotlessly clean kitchen table for a cup of Brooke Bond from the family's bone china tea service that would only be normally used once in a blue moon.

Mothers mind couldn't rest. The weight of endless chores she had put upon herself troubled her. Everything spun in her befuddled brain. She twitched in a hypnotic-like trance and an incomprehensible gibberish flowed from her distorted mouth.

Chapter 16: Sack the Chauffeur

As Brenda and Jim prepared to depart for the shops, Mother manoeuvred herself to close the creaky front door behind them. A gleaming white monster of a limousine glided to a halt behind the rusty old Hillman of Jim's. The three stood dumbstruck watching as the large driver's door swung open. The unmistakable figure of Gary appeared from the confines of this impressive Vauxhall Cresta.

Gary spoke, pointing to the huge vehicle that brightened up the dowdy grey street. "What d'you think of this then, madam? I had a chance to hire it from a mate of mine, so I thought just what we need to bring our Brian home in style."

He casually allowed the door to fall shut with a clunk and strode around the gigantic car towards the pavement. He'd really gone to town this time, to obtain the sought after affections of his future mother-in-law. He was well-pleased with the initial stunned expression on her pallid face. Not content with just the car to impress, Gary had dressed himself to match. He looked unusually fashionable in a brand new, light grey Italian-style suit. On his feet he wore black patent winkle pickers. Illuminous yellow tie and handkerchief contrasted with his Persil-white shirt. He adjusted the alignment of the small lapels on his box jacket and then glanced up at the exasperated Jim and winked triumphantly.

There existed a good-humoured rivalry between the two-prospective son-in-law's and was the source of many a comical interlude. I was always the obvious target to win over Mum's partiality and get into her good books, but not being a blood relation of the partisan Mother, made full acceptance impossible. From time to time they had fun trying though.

Mum ran her hands sensuously over the paintwork of the striking automobile. She looked up at Gary, now standing between Jim and Brenda in the open doorway. She smiled affectionately and spoke softly with a rare hint of sincerity: "You've done us proud, son. I shall always remember this."

Son! thought the surprised Gary. *Fine accolade indeed!* He turned just in time to watch Jim's face curdle to an envious green. He couldn't resist a satisfied smile to slightly show. "Well," replied Gary, still smarming with his pride, "I know how important today is to you, so there you are."

She patted him on the shoulder as she edged her way past them and back into the darkness of the hallway.

Gary turned to follow, wincing as a sharp pain stabbed into his left buttock.

Jim had pinched him hard and whispered into his ear, "You bloody creep-arse! This is war!"

Gary's sore bum made him limp slightly, but couldn't stop his pleasurable gloating inside.

The first round victory to Gary was costing Jim more money than he had intended to spend. He felt duty bound to fight back, so he lavishly purchased boxes of cakes, chocolates, a large basket of fresh fruit, and three football annuals.

Brenda, acknowledging the situation, helped towards the total cost. She couldn't allow Hilary's intended to pull one over on her loved one.

The thanks for this generosity was overshadowed by the good news being blurted out by Gary as he raced into the kitchen, having just returned from telephoning the hospital from the box on the corner. "Brian's coming home today!"

All the females cheered loudly and punched the air, ignoring poor old Jim who was still unpacking the shopping. *Oh balls!* he thought.

After endlessly willing the hands of the watch to move faster, it was time to leave.

Mum, helped by her three girls, was now wedged into her one and only wedding and funeral winter coat. A large royal blue velvet hat was placed onto her head and her nose was powdered for one last time. She grabbed her shiny black handbag that dangled from the wooden knob on the bannister. "Oh well, this is it. Come on Gary or we'll be late for getting there."

Gary hurried, making certain that he was first out of the house. He ran to open the rear door of the limo.

The approaching queen of the day nodded her approval and smiled. "Thank you, young sir!" she announced, before slipping gracefully into the comfortably upholstered bench seat.

Gary made sure that she and her clothing were well clear before carefully closing the door. Her usual fear of travel was easily brushed aside today. Nothing was going to stop her feeling like a million dollars. She regally waved to her onlooking family and then to the groups of pinney-clad neighbours that were congregated, gossiping with conjecture over what was going on at number forty-two.

Gary drove in total silence, not wishing to

break the act of the perfect chauffeur.

The journey passed all too quickly. Mum was lapping up the luxury.

Gary drew to a halt right outside the main entrance of the Bristol United Hospital, not in the least bit concerned about the large "no parking" signs. Once again, he fussed around, helping his precious cargo to her feet as she stepped out of her conveyance.

It was quite a walk to the third floor. Mother had learnt the hard way earlier that week that she needed to pace herself carefully or she would puff and pant for ages to get over it.

They unexpectedly found me in the ward day room. I was alone sitting on a grubby armchair that had been donated by the League of Friends. I was holding all my belongings on my lap in brown carrier bags.

Perched on top of a high table in the corner was a large black and white television. It was broadcasting a school's programme with a very loud echo.

"Hello my lover! Give you're old mum a big hug!"

My arms became helplessly trapped beneath the mountain of bags in front of me. I had no way of defending myself from the cold, wet gummy kisses from my elated mother.

"'Ello Mum, hello Gary, nice to see you," I said sarcastically, looking over Mum's shoulder as she cradled me passionately.

Gary gave me a wink, understanding my embarrassment.

Mum at last unravelled herself and straightened her crooked hat. She enquired with a sourness in her manner, "Why have you been shoved in 'ere, Bri, with all your stuff?"

I sniffed. "They wanted my bed for someone else, so they asked me if I minded waiting in 'ere, that's all."

I handed two of my carriers to Gary's willing outstretched hands.

"Well I think they all got a bloody cheek!" howled Mum, hoping someone employed by the hospital was within earshot.

"Shut up Mum! Let's just go home, eh?" I said, trying to quell her temper.

She clutched my hand tight and we left the poorly furnished room, still with the hippy-looking professor on the television explaining the theory of relativity.

As we made our way slowly along the artificially lit corridor, one of the young student nurses from ward twenty-three hurried past.

Mother recognised her and loudly called

after her. "Ohh! Ooh! Miss!"

The pretty dark haired girl spun round to see who was calling to her.

Mum unclasped her handbag and fished inside. She produced a half pound box of Quality Street and pushed it into the hands of the surprised nurse. "Here you are love. Share this out with the rest of you, and thank you all for what you've done for my little boy."

The bemused nurse took the chocolates, smiled, then continued on her way.

Gary and me smiled at each other, both harbouring the same thoughts. *Two-faced old cow!*

The red-faced hospital porter hollered as he pointed to the three feet high wooden signs dotted at ten feet intervals along the edge of the pavement. "Can't you bloody read?!"

Gary barked back, "Shut your face up, you miserable git!"

He placed the key into the car door and then Mum rattled, "It was an emergency." She pushed me gently into the back seat, then wriggled in beside me, nudging me over with her rump.

The little grey-coated terrier didn't like being ignored. He started shaking his fist and mouthing obscenities, hating the fact that his rollicking was being treated with such levity.

When the doors were securely closed and the engine fired up to a feline purr, Gary wound down the large window and as the car gracefully eased away from the curb, he poked his tongue out at the furious porter.

Mum said, "What a 'orrible little bloke!" pulling me towards her, wrapping her strong arm around my shoulders.

Gary kept an eye in the rear-view mirror until the seething hospital worker disappeared from sight.

I chuckled to myself as I looked up into Mother's heavily powdered wrinkled face. *Nothing changes*, I thought, *still the same common lot.*

Gary's deep voice broke the silence. "What d'you think of the car then, Bri? It's a belter, isn't it?"

I struggled to free myself from my mother's vice-like grip. I gazed around in admiration at the beautiful interior. "Yes, Gar, it's a belter all right. Where's get it from?"

As Gary began to explain the details of how he came by it for the day, a slight sensation of unevenness in the engine's running became noticeable. It gradually increased, becoming more and more violent, until we were being repeatedly thrown back and forth in our seats. The car eventually kangarooed to a spluttering halt.

A red-faced Gary turned in his seat and babbled apologetically, "I'm sorry, folks, I think we've broken down."

"Broken down!" screamed Mum through a crinkled frown.

"Yes," replied Gary sheepishly. "Just sit there and I'll have a look under the bonnet."

"I bet we don't just sit 'ere," hammered my increasingly anxious mother. "Go and ring up Mrs Evans at number thirty-six and get a message to our house. Jim can come and get us."

Gary reluctantly slunk off down the busy road, cursing under his breath.

Before he was out of earshot Mum had told him in no uncertain terms what she thought of him and his friend's unreliable heap of goat shit!

Jim could hardly contain himself as he received the words from the saggy-faced Mrs Evans at the front door.

"What you grinning' for?" snarled Brenda from her kneeling position in front of the half-cleaned oven.

Jim dived for his jacket that hung limply from the back of the chair. He stammered a reply as he fought back the laughter that was welling up deep inside him, "Guess what? It's . . . it's Gary! His fancy car has only gone and conked out on the Stapleford Road!"

"Oh no!" yelled Hilary as she ran from the back garden.

By now the figure of Jim had lost shape and control – he just lay spread-eagled on the kitchen table, tears rolling down his cheeks, giggling unrestrainedly.

As Hilary caught sight of his helpless frame, she shrieked disapprovingly, "I don't think it's bloody funny! What can you see to laugh at?"

Slowly Jim peeled himself from the table top and stood upright, whimpering and clutching his aching sides as he attempted to stifle his chuckling. "No, no, you're right. I'll er, I'll go and rescue them," he said, still failing to completely compose himself. He quickly threw on his coat and ran out, not daring to glance back, knowing that to hang around much longer will have produced an inevitable thump from Hilary.

He didn't need to look hard to find us. The unmistakable shape of a white Cresta brought him to an abrupt standstill. Jim proudly walked from his humble Hillman Minx and strode towards the out-of-service vehicle.

The sound of knocking and banging rang out from beneath the angled bonnet as Gary fought desperately to fix it.

"Come on, Mrs Wilson, let's get Brian home," said Jim as he drew close.

The sudden sound of his voice made Gary spring up, banging his head hard on the heavy bonnet.

"Sorry Gary! Didn't see you there 'ard at work. Is there anything' I can do?"

Gary's greasy splattered face appeared from its confines and through clenched teeth he snarled so only Jim could hear, "Yes, there is. Piss off!"

Gloria caught sight of them turning into their road through the front room window. The welcoming committee moved pensively out onto the pavement just as the rusty old Hillman screeched to an abrupt stop.

The substitute chauffeur proudly ran to help me and my dishevelled mother from the cramped confines of the back seat. Mother straightened herself up and as expected wore a face like thunder. She angrily pushed them all aside as she menacingly stamped into the house, leaving the three girls to cuddle and welcome me for themselves.

They guided me carefully through the sombre lit hallway towards the open kitchen door. We knew it was time to face Mum, sensing that the car breaking down was sure to have shattered her illusion of the perfect day. The girls feared it might take weeks for her malice-ridden body to not only forgive Gary, but also the world.

Gloria cowardly pushed me in first, anticipating that I would be least likely to be scorned. All three daughters held back waiting for Mum's reaction before attempting to infiltrate her space. They were pleasantly surprised to hear a meek voice greet me.

"All right my darling? How you feeling after that ordeal? Still, let's not think any more about it, eh?"

She placed a caring arm around my shoulder and plonked a slobbery kiss right in the middle of my forehead.

"Bloody hell! What a turn up," whispered Hilary to her confused sisters. "It must 'ave turned her head having our Bri away from here!"

They sluggishly entered the kitchen, all avoiding eye contact with Mum. What an unpredictable woman!

Chapter 17: Down Memory Lane

Mother seemed to have shrugged off the Cresta incident with a worrying ease. She appeared calm and deliriously happy, skipping around making sure that the gas was lit under the kettle, then producing a plateful of delicately coloured Fancy Cakes from the top shelf of the grubby old free-standing pantry.

"Come on, my lovelies, let's sit down and 'ave a cake to celebrate my baby being home again, where he belongs."

I understood Mum's curious upbeat mood more than the rest because, like her, I had the ability to affect a mental block when things looked stacked up against happiness. I knew that this was actually what was happening now in her troubled mind. The only problem was, although it was possible in the short-term to numb your true feelings of anger and despair, it would lurk there, close to the surface, and without warning reveal itself when least expected.

After a feast of a lunch, we nestled into the comparative comfort of our best front room. Most working-class homes that have a female influence have a room like this – an unused, tacky showpiece of a museum full of fairground ornaments and gaudy trinkets collected over many decades, all displayed on well-polished shelves. In the centre was a rarely sat on flowery, cottage-style three-piece suite.

Today was exceptional. Everyone was welcomed into Mum's lavender-smelling mausoleum. I felt quite the celebrity, and really flattered by all this.

From an early age all four of us had instinctively found ways of directing Mum's complicated mind from menacing thoughts. The easiest and most rewarding was to subtly bring the conversation around to what it must have been like to live through the Second World War.

Mum's wartime memories were priceless and although we had heard the same tales over and over, we never tired of them. When Mother's thoughts began to drift back to distant days, her whole being seemed more spirited. Her eyes would sparkle with the impishness of youth and the facial lines brought about by the frowns of everyday stresses looked less noticeable, revealing glimpses of a once attractive girl.

The vivid stories never failed to enthral all four of us.

As Mum's mind wandered through harrowing and heart-warming times, the sense of comradeship and love always came shining through. A warped feeling of genuine envy of Mum's adventures welled up inside me. It was hard to comprehend that battling through six years of poverty-stricken hell could now be remembered with a strange fondness.

We would all sit in silence, hanging on every word. Laughing when Mum would laugh and gasping openly with her as distress and sadness brought a quiver to her lip and a glaze to her eyes.

Goading these reminiscences out had to be handled very delicately, otherwise you were in grave danger of pushing her thoughts too far back, back to a devastatingly unhappy childhood which she shared with her two sisters and two brothers. They lived an unbelievably tortured existence with an ageing, bad-tempered alcoholic of a father and schizophrenic mother, who became so mentally unbalanced that every day seemed an uphill struggle to survive. You could tell by Mum's panic-stricken face when chilling recollections of those horrific days were returning to haunt her.

We had all learned of Mum's ghastly upbringing from our Uncle Bert at a family party. Somehow, he had got through it all with fewer lasting mental scars. He graphically enlightened us on how our deranged grandmother had ended her sad life prematurely in a bleak mental institution.

Prior to this, Mum, aged only eleven, had miraculously battled to protect herself and the four smaller vulnerable children from the long periods of violent aggression from their unpredictable mother.

Their work-shy father spent every day on his own mission of destruction, begging, borrowing or stealing any form of strong liquor to binge on, leaving him either unconscious or even worse, in a scathing vicious rage.

The poor innocent children had only the protection of the frail Joyce to save them from life-threatening actions.

The two rented rooms of abject squalor above the small dairy gave no space to hide from the foreboding atmosphere that surrounded them and the evil stench of immorality that children should be spared from.

Every evening held the same ritual. Father would be sprawled across an armchair with Mother sitting squinting at the words she had feverishly jotted down into a small black notebook by the feeble flame of a smelly oil lamp. Mum would try to make the others as comfortable as possible on the damp floor of the other room, trying to coax them to sleep before the inevitable stirring of their drunken brute of a father.

Loud abuse would quickly turn to a bloody fight between the deranged parents, only finally coming to a grim conclusion when Father had pinned down the pathetic female form and forced all of his animal-like pleasures onto her until he would grunt aloud like a bear with primeval satisfaction.

Mum would virtually smother the children as the barbaric acts took place, desperately attempting to prevent frightened screams from reaching their parents' depraved ears.

When all that could be heard was the fretful weeping of the bruised and defiled mother, Mum would only then try to control her own petrified young body, holding her little family close as she rocked and cried until sleep came.

As the cheerless winter days become shorter, Mum sensed that her mother's latest depression was deeper and more serious. She now paid little attention to her children, except to strike out at them and mumble incomprehensibly. She never bothered to dress now and just wandered the unswept rooms with a vacant, sallow expression, clutching her precious diary, squeezing it so tightly that her knuckles strained white.

A rare unwelcomed visit from their father's mother heralded changes in their harrowing existence. The declining health and sanity of their mother was blatantly obvious to her and the unwashed hungry state of the children were too much to be ignored. Reluctantly, the shocked grandmother informed the family GP of the worrying family situation. A hasty visit from him just to confirm matters for himself was enough to set the wheels quickly in motion. Then, their mother was promptly carted off by the men in white coats.

Father gave no resistance as his mother collected the sparse belongings of the children and took them with her to a less daunting life the other side of town.

Their mother's health declined rapidly in the overcrowded asylum and within three months she was dead.

Their puzzled father was now free to pickle his liver twenty-four hours a day. Without his wife to abuse, he didn't last long before he was discovered drowned on his own vomit.

The full extent of the macabre mind of our grandmother was only fully explained when Mum visited the longstanding family GP at the age of nineteen. He had found her mother's little black book when he attended the family flat to confirm the death of her father. The sadness and suffering in her mother's tortured mind almost tore her heart out. Mum shivered as an icy chill engulfed her as she read of her mother's plan to murder all the five children and then commit suicide herself.

A mixture of feelings gripped her. Relief that they had been rescued before the event, but also a strange sense of guilt that her mother had to die alone. She now understood that in a morbid, twisted way, her mother had loved her children so much that she wanted to spare them from the cruel pessimistic world that she had to endure.

The afternoon light was now beginning to fade. The shadows lengthen and bring a sombre glow to the room.

Mum, begrudgingly, brought her session of "down memory lane" to a close.

Chapter 18: Home-coming Blues

I sprang forward in my chair, yawned, stretched my arms aloft and spoke: "I hate to be a party pooper but, sorry folks, I'm not used to all this hectic home life. It's all made me quite weary."

I was already getting to my feet and making my way to the door.

Mother smiled, her face back once again carrying the burdens of the ageing process and her wrinkles deeply etched on her worn complexion. "All right my little pet, you get on up to bed and I'll bring you up a cuppa."

Not another bloody of cup of tea, I thought, as I lowered my head respectfully to everybody before making my exit. If I had to drink any more tea I'll be piddling all night!

I trudged wearily with lead-filled legs up the narrow stairway towards the sanctuary of my box bedroom. Once inside, I backed myself clumsily against the door to shut it. I breathed deeply through my nose and the strong scent of beeswax did nothing to disguise the familiar sourness of damp and decay.

My fatigued state made me feel quite lightheaded and my legs were like jelly. I slumped clumsily onto the bed and sat for several seconds with my hands clasped to my face endeavouring to collect my thoughts. My tired eyes reluctantly began to survey the small room, stopping automatically on my beloved record player and the two feet high pile of crumpled record sleeves standing precariously alongside it. Instinctively, I jumped up, reaching out for the comfort of holding my cherished collection. I carefully scooped them up and gently placed them beside me. My subconscious mind was already one step ahead of my frantic fingertips. I skipped through the cardboard covers feverishly searching for the one and only priceless "Tears of a Clown". I found my favourite about three quarters of the way down the tattered and torn stack. I tutted loudly, really put out that someone whilst tidying had re-arranged their order. Tears of a Clown should always be pride of place on top. I felt the strong need and desire to experience the unique emotions that only that song could evoke.

The unpleasant mixture of smells and the claustrophobic confines of my bedroom now mattered not. I tenderly straightened the bent corners of the well-worn cover and stared with tunnelled concentration at the song title written in large black letters. Not since the night that now seemed light years away, when

I had suffered at the hands and boots of Hardy and Kuzeki, had these unsettling and disorientating feelings ran through me. My sadness and yearning for Diane Lewis was real again. No longer could I hide in the insular world of physical healing. These tortured wanton sensations hurt a thousand times more than the pains inflicted by the attack.

Once more the restrictions of my domestic straight jacket were suffocating me. The conflict of wanting to share my life and fulfil my potential with Diane versus the grim reality of the out-of-bounds barrier that tore at my soul.

Having put all the records neatly back, I touched one last time the top and most treasured one, before collapsing with a bump onto my squeaky mattress. My confused mind, with all of its unanswerable thoughts, whirled and throbbed.

Eventually I slipped into the comparative escapism of a shallow, jumpy sleep.

During the next few days, my lethargic and melancholy demeanour was blamed by the family on a delayed shock reaction to my beating.

They all took turns to sit with me, trying to cheer me up and break the cloud of doom that hovered close. Nothing seemed to work, with no signs of the insurmountable pessimism lifting at all.

Mum became increasingly concerned with my lifeless form and wept openly whenever she brought my meals and witnessed my sorry state.

By the fourth day the whole family were in total despair. My depression was now rubbing off onto everyone and short tempers and constant bickering flared at every opportunity.

Brenda's temper was on the shortest fuse and after a row erupted between Gloria and Hilary about whose turn it was to wash up, Brenda leapt up and screamed, "Right, that's it! I've 'ad enough of this pussyfooting around. I can't take anymore. Can't you see what he's doing to us?"

"What's on about?" questioned Mum.

"He needs a bloody good talking to, selfish little git he is. As long as we feel sorry for him, he'll carry on. Well, I've 'ad it with him."

She bounced out of the kitchen with the fretting mother close on her heels. "Bren! Don't do anything silly."

Brenda turned. "Stay here, Mum, I know what I'm doing."

Mum was frozen to the spot, struck motionless by her daughter's forthright manner.

The enraged plump teenager stormed up the stairs and into my bedroom, slamming the door behind her. I was still in the horizontal position that I had taken up for the last sixty hours, except for excursions to the lavatory. The bedroom floor was littered with discarded books and comics. My face still carried the all-too-familiar empty expression, with inanimate eyes fixed rigidly towards the crumbling ceiling. The unpleasant aroma of my unwashed body filled the room. Now face-to-face with me, and seeing that I was so obviously at serious odds with the world, Brenda's anger weakened. When she spoke her tone was only that of a concerned loved one.

"What's the trouble with you, love? You know we rely on you to keep us going."

I focused on the towering figure above me. "I'm ill! That's what's wrong with me, ill."

"That was last week," retorted Brenda. "This week it's sommat else. You know I can always tell when you're bottling things up."

I sighed as I pushed my head harder into my pillow. It was true enough. Brenda had always been able to understand my feelings and emotions far more than anyone else. But this was one problem that no amount of talking about would solve.

She spoke again in a firm but kindly tone: "I know you think I'm centuries older than you, but give me a chance, bend my ear a bit."

I managed a strained smile, appreciating my sister's gallant efforts but, how could I? Even if I had wanted to share my suicidal feelings with someone, she was part of my embarrassments and troubled existence.

Brenda now realised that this depressed state would not allow sensible conversation, so she walked towards the door, turning for one last comment. "Well anyway, when you feel ready Bri, let me try and help. In the meantime, start looking on the bright side. Get up, get on with it! Your hair looks like you could fry chips in it and your teeth got 'alf inch of fur on 'em! Get your act together or you'll rot."

The room fell silent again and I breathed deeply as I digested my sister's words of wisdom. I reached across to the rickety bedside cabinet, picked up a small handled mirror – it was part of a brush and comb set given to me by Uncle Bert. I wiped the dusty glass into my bedspread before holding it close to my face. *Oh my Gawd!* I shrieked, horrified at my ghastly appearance. My eyes were sunken and grey, my lips and nose still sported dark scabs just ready for picking. My chin and pyjamas were speckled with debris of a week's sloppy eating. My Beatles-style haircut was now stuck to my head in unkempt shiny wedges. *She's right about one thing. . . I do look a bloody mess!*

I placed the mirror back where it belonged, pulled my bedclothes up high around my ears, turned onto my side and went fast asleep.

Chapter 19: The Breakfast from Hell

My mother woke me at nine o'clock with my breakfast held precariously in front of her on an old wicker tray. I heaved myself into a semi-sitting position and turned my pillow long ways to support my back.

"You look chirpier this morning, my love."

"That's cos it's Saturday, I expect."

She placed my fat-laden fry-up in front of me.

"Oh you know, Mum, can't keep a good man down."

Mum grinned a gummy grin and spoke cheerfully: "That's better, my baby, that's what I want to 'ear."

She then left me in peace to devour my mouth-watering meal.

Most people have a unique ritual way of eating a fried breakfast. My tried and trusted method, although lacking any form of etiquette or table manners, served its purpose in getting the contents from my plate into my stomach in two minutes' flat. I started by lavishly pouring tomato ketchup into pretty spiral patterns over the egg, bacon and sausages. Next, I laid a heavily buttered doorstep of crusty bread onto the flat of my left hand. I then proceeded with finger and thumb to heap rasher after rasher of dripping bacon onto one half of the bread. When the desired amount, usually five or six, were in place, grease, melted butter and sauce were in great danger of dripping everywhere. I would then quickly and firmly clap the mountainous sandwich together. Leaning forward over my plate the main object now was to see how much of the colourful mess I could put into mouth before it completely lost its form and disintegrated into a heap needing to be mopped up with a knife and fork at a later stage. The repulsive-looking edible "mouth organ" was now ready. With an imaginary roll on the drums, my wide-open mouth descended on its prey. I bit and chewed on the bulky mouthful with a rapid, chomping motion. I knew from past experience that streaky bacon, if not taken cautiously, had a tendency to try and slip past your tonsils lengthways causing choking. That knowledge wasn't enough to deter me from my grotesque style of banqueting. Having bitten off more than was comfortable to chew, I relaxed my head back whilst my mouth wrestled with the tasty gobful. I purred with consummate ecstasy as the salty tomato-flavoured concoction delighted my taste buds. After much tongue manoeuvring and noisy gulping, the first mouthful was near to being conquered. I opened my eyes wide and swallowed with relish.

I vaguely heard muffled sounds of raised voices drifting up from downstairs. I momentarily ceased my chewing and pricked up my ears trying to make sense of the increasing commotion. The unmistakable clip clop of hasty footsteps grew louder as they neared my bedroom.

As the hollow paces abruptly halted, Gloria's makeup-laden physog appeared. Her moon-shaped face beamed with excitement. She stammered to convey her message. "Bri! Bri! Get yourself ready, you've got a visitor."

She slammed the door to my room shut, then, in all of a fluster, bounced back down the stairs.

I was taken aback by the sudden intrusion and quizzed my mind rapidly to ascertain the identity of my unexpected and unwanted guest. My thoughts slowed as I sorted the possibilities out in my head. It can only be either Steve or Geoff, I decided. I bet they've come to get the latest gossip on my injuries or, worse still, come to nick my sausages. *Well that's one thing that I can certainly stop happening*, I thought, grabbing the two slippery bangers off my plate. I rammed them unceremoniously sideways into my cavernous mouth. The local butcher's speciality pork and beef sausages stayed whole, stretching my cheeks out sideways, making me appear like an hamster with the mumps. My sharp wit was already hatching a plan to play on my school chums. I'd pretend that the food-induced swellings to my face was all part of my beating. I fought to close my mouth and screwed my eyes up into an exaggerated pained expression.

It was what seemed an age before to my surprise a polite knock at my door broke the silence. I suddenly felt quite uneasy. This didn't seem to be the style for Steve or Geoff. They had never knocked on a door in their entire life. Watching intently as the old wooden door opened, a coldness swept across me. My life had always seemed to be ill-fated with a constant series of humiliating episodes. The next few moments were to unfold into the very pinnacle of absolute embarrassment and far and away the top of the long list of ultimate degradations.

The bedroom door swung its course with a slow metallic creak and already the icy sixth sense pre-warning of imminent perils had struck me. What seemed to be a hugely funny joke a couple of seconds ago was now an enormous serious liability in my throat. I coughed and spluttered as I gagged on the now unwanted food that semi-blocked my windpipe. Then, there she stood. The unrivalled majesty of Diane Lewis, unfittingly framed by a dirty yellow doorway. She stood gazing inquisitively into my shambolic bedroom. My eyes were affixed with terror. The complexities of this belittling situation painfully started to hit home. There was no hole to crawl into or self-destruction button to press. A bizarre feeling of raw nakedness made me twitch repeatedly. The search for any hope of pretence was futile. *What the hell was she doing crossing the million-mile void into my shameful world?* I wished she would somehow disappear and go back to perfect, stylish planet where she belonged.

The cold, inhospitable reception didn't deter her caring nature and the object of her intentions. Diane smiled sweetly at me. I allowed the remnants of my colossal buttie to fall from my grip and hit the rough wooden tray with a plop. I nervously wiped my chin of all grease onto the sleeve of my grubby striped pyjamas.

Diane spoke and goose pimples developed, tightening my already creeping skin. "I hope you don't mind me coming to see you. I really felt I 'ad to."

I managed a feeble nod, not yet ready to

attempt a tangible reply.

Diane looked deep into my forlorn, troubled face, concerned that I would be blaming her for being the cause of my cruel beating.

"I know the reason why you were attacked. It was because you protected me at the careers evening, wasn't it? I really am very sorry."

Not even in this befuddled state could I allow this girl, who meant everything to me, to feel in any way guilty for the attack on me. I coughed aloud to clear my throat before proclaiming her innocence. "Oh no! Don't be daft! They were looking to give it to somebody that night and big mouth here gave them a good excuse." I finished with a forgiving wink that was met with an affectionate grin from a very relieved Diane.

Now the initial fears and barriers were slightly less, I began to feel more able to enjoy the company of the girl I adored, but not for one second could I forget my tramp-like appearance and my shabby family and surroundings that would always alienate me from this quite perfect being.

Diane spoke again. "Oh well, can't stop long I'm afraid. My dad's outside waiting for me in the car."

I noticed the blonde girl's eyes stray towards my record collection. Her gaze dwelt for a while as she read the one visible song title.

"You've got good taste. That's my favourite."

She glided close to me and bashfully patted the back of my hand with hers. All this was far too much for me. I lowered my head close to tears and stared right through the now congealing half-eaten breakfast. I couldn't even bring myself to acknowledge Diane's farewell. She left the door ajar and without a sound she walked away and down the stairs.

The thunderous stomping of my family's feet brought my shell-shocked head back into gear. Without the radiance of Diane my little box bedroom seemed dowdier than ever. I vented my pent-up self-pity by shoving the tray from my lap and crushing it thoughtlessly onto the floor. Luckily the plate and sauce bottle were better tempered than me and they stayed whole.

Chapter 20: My Sister Understands

My wide-eyed curious family herded themselves into my small room. As they jostled for position, they gawped at me with subnormal expressions. They all spoke at once, gabbling question after question to me.

The first that was audible belonged to Hilary. "What a lovely girl, Bri. Why haven't you told us about her?"

I grimaced as I placed my hand firmly over my ears, trying to blank out the barrage of raised voices.

I replied with a shout, not out of anger, but attempting to make myself heard. "Nothin' to tell. She's just a friend from school."

As the inquisitive grilling continued, my face glowed to a deep pink as an attention-provoked blush rose up.

Mum was next to drill a comprehensible poser to me. "What's 'er name, Bri? I've never seen such a good-looking lass. Not like they Rocks or Modder's that you hear about."

The girls all at once stopped their babbling, interested to hear their brother's answer to Mother's malapropped enquiry.

"'Er name is Diane Lewis. I've only known

'er about three weeks, and you're right, Mum, she isn't a Mod or a Rocker."

My visual growing uneasiness was enough to show all of my family that Diane Lewis meant more to me than at this stage I would be willing to divulge.

Brenda was first to react to my awkwardness. She cleverly edged the rest out of my room before closing the door behind them, leaving her alone with me.

I appreciated Brenda's thoughtfulness and with a huge sigh of relief uttered, "Thanks, Bren. I thought my brain was going to explode then."

Brenda smiled as she perched herself precariously at the foot of my bed. "I think it's time for our little chat now, don't you Bruv?"

I shrugged my shoulders and sank a little deeper into my bedclothes, searching for warmth as a comfort.

"I don't know what to say, Bren, I really don't."

She placed her hand on one of the lumps in the bedclothes, then waggled my blanket-covered foot quite firmly. "Can't you understand, Brian? You don't need to say anythin'. We've all been through what you're going through, and we know how much it hurts." Brenda leant forward and spoke softly in case eavesdroppers were at the door. "Did you know our Mum farted as I introduced her to my first boyfriend?"

I clenched my teeth together to stifle a smile.

"It's true. And then there was the time the vicar came around and the cat crapped in his trilby!"

"You're kiddin'?" I giggled, suddenly feeling liberated from my embarrassments.

Brenda stood upright and folded her arms around her ample bosom, taking up the gossiping-over-the-garden-wall stance.

My funny bone was now well and truly tickled and I rocked with laughter. Brenda giggled with me, more out of a sense of achievement at having, at long last, found common ground to bring out my wicked sense of humour. She noticed the devilish sparkle back in my eye, the one that the whole household had been so badly missing. Brenda shuffled forward and placed both hands tenderly onto my shoulders. The sound of my laughter ceased as suddenly as it had started. We found ourselves staring deeply into each other's eyes, almost trying to delve into one another's souls. As my joyful expression dropped, a dark saddening feeling replaced it. Tears rose to sting my eyes. Instinctively, Brenda drew me close and rocked me rhythmically as she cradled my head and neck. My breathing changed to a convulsive jerk as I sobbed.

Brenda whispered to me as she smoothed back my bedraggled fringe from my emotion-ridden face. "Shhh, shhh, come on, it will all be all right, you'll see."

After several minutes had passed, and lots of words of comfort, Brenda felt my weight change within her grasp and a less stressful tone in my breathing, as if in slow motion she gently laid me back carefully, releasing her arms from behind me. My sleep had taken control. She kissed my sweaty forehead, before silently creeping from my room.

Chapter 21: Match Makers

"Crack" went the letterbox flap as the strong spring slapped it shut. Brenda looked up in time to watch a slip of paper float to the floor and rest print downwards on the frayed coconut mat. She jumped down the last few stairs and made her way towards it picking up the flimsy note. She read. Southleaze School was apparently having their annual pupils' disco the following Monday evening. All pupils welcome.

Brenda's mind was working overtime. *I've certainly never seen a note such as this personally delivered before*, she pondered. Maybe one of the teachers had taken it upon themselves to invite Brian or maybe it was his beloved Diane trying in a way to nudge the arm of fate. *I hope it is*, she thought.

Then there's the dreadful possibility. Could it be the gang that beat our Brian up trying to line him up for another kicking? No, that was too horrible to contemplate. She promised herself that she would keep any negative thoughts like that well under wraps. She decided that this disco could be exactly what her brother needed to shake off his agoraphobic and self-pitying tendencies.

"What are you looking so chuffed about?"

enquired Gloria from behind a thousand calories of chocolate éclair.

Brenda strode into the kitchen waving the note above her head. She edged herself into a chair between Mother and Hilary who, like Gloria, was seriously engaged in devouring their Saturday morning treat from the local cake shop. The crockery on the table all tinkled as Brenda slapped the school invite down in front of them.

Gloria's reactions were quickest as she snatched it up, leaving her floundering mother and sister grasping at thin air.

"Watch what you're doing!" shrieked Brenda. "You're covering it in cream and chocolate."

Gloria sucked her fingers loudly one by one and attempted to wipe the smears off of the paper with her cardigan sleeve.

"Give it 'ere, you messy cow!" growled Brenda, gripping it from the clutches of Gloria. "Right," she demanded, "listen to this, it's important." She held the printed sheet with both hands and read it as if it was a royal proclamation.

The expected dramatic response didn't materialise and as Brenda finished her recital, all her female audience did was shrug their shoulders and carry on with their sweet feast.

"What were we supposed to make of that

then?" asked a nonplussed Hilary.

Brenda waved the piece of paper so close to Hilary's nose it made her blink. "Listen you lot, our Bri's up there feeling love-sick and sorry for himself, and we all know how that feels."

Mother scratched the back of her head and wrinkled up her nose trying to understand the significance of Brenda's outburst.

Gloria fought with words through a mouthful of doughnut. "Oh, I get it, you think he ought to go. Is that it?"

Brenda placed her hands firmly onto her ample hips and tutted loudly. "Well done, bird brain! That's exactly what I'm sayin'. Don't you think it's a good idea?"

All three daughters watched as Mum noticeably adopted her anxious pose and developed her lifelong instinct for squashing any such adventure away from her watchful care.

The three girls simultaneously turned their heads to glare at their mother's anguish, their disapproving eyes making her feel quite uncomfortable and weak against the household's diplomatic state.

She slumped back into her chair and sighed, a defeated woman but with a weird sense of pride and a realisation that all her children were growing into caring and forthright adults, despite their claustrophobic childhood, where their mother's tragic and insecure upbringing had tempered her way of parenting, believing that overprotecting and smothering equalled love. For the very first time she acknowledged that it didn't. To have offspring that were self-sufficient and worldly-wise was a wonderful accomplishment. A peaceful warm glow of self-satisfaction enveloped her.

Brenda excitedly scuffed the chair legs across the floor and moved closer to the table. "Here's my plan," she said. "Bri's in love and don't think he's good enough for her. Do we agree?"

Gloria wiped her chin of dribbled cream. "So what!" she mumbled.

Mum and Hilary frowned at Gloria's flippant comment.

"Carry on, my love," ordered Mum. "Forget about that ignorant cow!"

Gloria poked out a cake-speckled tongue as Brenda continued.

"He's so down, I don't think he'll ever get up from his bed unless we give 'im a bloody good shove."

"'Ow can we do that then?" enquired Hilary. "He doesn't want to know anythin'."

Brenda replied, "Diane Lewis, that's his reason. We got to make sure he's in with a chance with her."

These thought-provoking remarks were enough to stimulate a family debate as they all thrashed out their opinions and eventually decided on the best course of action: To goad their brother into attending the school disco, where they were all pretty sure Diane would be there, hopefully waiting for him.

Keeping their master plan from me for as long as possible was a must knowing my present mood. I would 1) hate their interference into his affairs, and 2) see all their efforts as a waste of time and destined for failure.

"He will need new clothes – something Mod," said Gloria.

"Yeah! And a new haircut," added Hilary.

"We'll all put together," announced Brenda, becoming more and more enthralled with the project.

A compromise about my hairstyle had to be met to appease Mother. "I don't mind it short, but not a bloody skinhead, eh?" requested Mum, pleased to be able to input into this scheme.

Hilary, who was once trained to be a hairdresser, was given the responsibility for that part of the makeover.

"What's the time?" asked Brenda.

"Nearly 'alf past one," barked Mum.

"This afternoon's the only chance we've got to get 'im a new outfit," remarked Brenda. "Jim's coming around at two, I'll get 'im to take us into town."

"I'll come an' all," said Hilary.

"And me!" shouted Gloria.

"I'll stay here and get tea ready by the time you all get home," added Mum, content with her contribution to events.

Gloria came up with a valid point. "'Ang on, 'ow can we get clothes for 'im upstairs if we don't know what's gonna fit him?"

"Oh shit! 'Ant thought of that," shrieked Brenda, fearing that the intended plot was about to fall apart.

"You've all got tape measures 'aint you?" chirped in Mum. "Go upstairs and size 'im up. He won't know what it's for."

After clumsily rummaging in all of the kitchen's many drawers, the three girls produced brightly coloured dressmaking measures and laid them in a heap on the middle of the table.

Mother, with a deft swoop, picked up the royal blue measure that belonged to Gloria. "What's up with this one?" she sarcastically asked as she unravelled its lengths between her outstretched hands. "Why is the first thirty inches stretched to twice its normal length?"

Gloria stumbled as she tried to snatch it

away from the scrutiny of her mother.

Hilary blocked her and carried on examining the elongated tape.

Gloria's cheeks reddened noticeably as she hollered, "Give it back! None of your bloody business!"

Brenda called out as understanding clicked into place: "I know what she's doin'. All that crap about her vital statistics! It's no wonder, is it, cheating cow!"

Gloria sat head in hands whilst the rest collapsed with laughter. They all recollected how only the day before watching Gloria parade through the house thrusting her midriff in everyone's faces, bringing their attention to the impressive twenty-six inch waist that was verified by the end of the royal blue measure imprisoning her wobbly stomach.

Mother desperately tried to compose herself, not wishing for the teasing to get out of hand. "Come on, that's enough," she encouraged, "we've got work to do." She placed a consoling hand on Gloria's shoulder, smiling at the dejected figure.

"Yes, let's get ready to pounce," mumbled the depleted Gloria.

Brenda gave her indication that the mickey-taking was over by announcing two tapes would be adequate to complete their task.

"D'you think we can do it when he's

asleep?" questioned Hilary.

"We can 'ave a go," replied Brenda.

"Creep up and make sure he's out for the count."

A minute later the twenty-six-inch-waisted girl was giving the thumbs-up sign to her two accomplices as they waited in silence below in the hallway.

Gloria held back the bedroom door as the sisters gingerly crept up the stairs and disappeared without a sound into the little box bedroom. With military precision they set about their objective.

Gloria stood one side of the bed, Brenda the other. In perfect synchronisation they gripped and slowly eased the bedclothes down revealing their shabby, pyjama-clad brother. They froze statue-like as I began to stir and waited whilst in my slumber I scratched my genitals and stretched, before lying still once again.

They waited for a few extra seconds before indicating to each other with elaborate gestures the best way to begin. My legs and body length were comparatively easy to assess. The hard bit was when they cautiously endeavoured to push the tape under my back. As if in slow motion, they drew both ends around to the front, mentally noting their findings. Just as they attempted to manoeuvre the measure from between me and the bed, I began to turn and mumble loudly, neatly trapping the arms of the two elder sisters. They gazed at each other across the bed in horror and disbelief.

Gloria's spark of inspiration rescued the situation. She plucked a loose feather that protruded from the pillow and proceeded to gently waggle it under her sleeping brother's nostrils. My nose twitched, I raised a hand to flick at the irritation and this caused my whole body to slightly move involuntarily, enough for Hilary and Brenda to gratefully retrieve their arms quickly from captivity.

Hilary nodded towards the door feeling that they had pushed their luck far enough. She leant over and briskly gathered the blankets back up over me, before scrambling back out of the room with her two sisters right behind her.

Returning to the kitchen they made themselves a nerve-calming cup of tea and of course a piece of bread pudding.

Upstairs I was stirring. *What a 'orrible nightmare!* I thought. *I must be more depressed than I thought. Fancy dreaming about being measured for your coffin, by your own family an' all.*

A cold shudder ran through me as morbid despair saddened me.

Chapter 22: Fashion Gurus

The busy town centre was buzzing with its usual army of deranged Saturday shoppers, most loaded down with enough provisions to cope with the great famine.

The Wilson girls were on a mission as they jostled and weaved a careful route avoiding a constant flow of oncoming zombies.

Jim sauntered aimlessly the length of a cricket pitch behind them, kicking the air as he trudged along, totally miffed at being seconded to help in this latest hair-brained scheme. Saturday afternoons usually meant a couple of bottles of Double Diamond, feet up, watching wrestling on the telly. *What a bleeding drag!* he fumed.

They all knew intimately the name of the clothes shop they were searching for. God knows their brother had rammed it down their throats at every opportunity. So-and-so from school had just bought a shirt from Astons, somebody else had a new coat from Astons. It was amazing how Mod you could look, even if you took your football boots to school in an Astons carrier bag. Up until today, all I could boast about was a couple of pairs of socks from the revered boutique, but in a few moments, all that would change.

They waited patiently for the queue of onlooking shoppers to move away from the large colourful display window before standing side-by-side gazing intently from one well-dressed dummy to another. It was quite breath-taking to witness the artistic way their stylish designs were merchandised. Quite rapidly it became apparent that none of them had a clue what I would choose if I were there with them.

"What d'you think, Glor?" asked Brenda. "You're the nearest to his age."

"Don't put the responsibility on me!" she howled. "It all looks bloody silly!"

Before a fully blown argument could erupt, their attentions were drawn to a gangly, spotty youth who was proudly strutting out of the double doors of the shop, swinging his two Astons carrier bags proudly. It was obvious to all that this adolescent was about the similar age to me and very obviously, a money-no-object dedicated follower of fashion.

Hilary was first to grab the moment. "Oy, you, hang on a minute!" she commanded.

The startled lad glanced round. To his shock and horror he saw three shady-looking, overweight women vigorously beckoning him towards them.

"Oh shit!" he wailed, already hurriedly running for it, dodging and darting in and out of the baffled pedestrians.

"Stop! Stop!" shouted Gloria as she started after him as best she could in her black patent stilettoes.

Her sisters were right there with her. The pallid-faced, bewildered youth periodically halted, looked back over his shoulder, then seeing that the tubby trio were on his heels kept running as if his life depended on it. He didn't have a clue what he had supposed to have done, but he felt guilty anyway, so he just kept on going.

When he stopped for a fourth time to catch his breath and assess the progress of his unlikely pursuers, he inadvertently brushed past an unsuspecting passer-by. He lost the grip of a carrier bag, sending it falling to the pavement beside him. He quickly bent over to retrieve it as an elderly stout gentleman with a walking stick barged into the back of him, sending him sprawling face down onto the cold concrete slabs. The old boy responsible was completely unrepentant and merrily carried along on his way without missing a step. The despairing lad instinctively rolled onto his back and was confronted by a jungle of legs and feet belonging to mindless shoppers trudging relentlessly around him, over him and through him. Huge human shadows eclipsed the sunlight from the petrified teenager.

Suddenly, he became aware of three pairs of chubby, stocking-covered calves imprisoning him. His impulse was to resist as they clumsily helped him to his feet. As the tussle ensued, he found himself engulfed by mounds of female flesh.

"I aint done nothin'!" he blurted with a pant.

"We know you haven't," apologised Brenda. "Didn't mean to scare you."

Now that he had been exonerated from any wrongdoing, his self-confidence grew into a stroppy brashness. "Then why were you dopey gits chasing me?" He bellowed.

Hilary lowered her face close to his and growled, "Less of your lip, you cheeky bleeder! All we wanted to know is what you're wearing."

The confused boy straightened his jacket and roughly brushed dirt from the knees of his light green trousers. Although still battling to comprehend what on earth this was all about, his quick-thinking determined that somehow, if he was clever, there could potentially be a bit of an earner in all of this. "It will cost you," he coyly remarked, his slanted smile attempting to convey an age above his obvious tender years, "for me time and trouble, like," he added reluctantly.

All three paid the pint-sized conman a pound each before he would divulge the trade names and styles of the garments he wore. "This is a Ben Sherman shirt," he boasted, "and this is Stay Press trousers. My jacket is a Harrington."

"And what are they things on your feet?" enquired Brenda.

"They're my Brogues," he bragged, lifting a foot high for their closer inspection.

"That'll do," howled Gloria. "Come on, let's back to the shop."

"Did that just happen?" muttered the bemused fashion magnet as he scratched his bristly head. He felt for the three one pound notes in his pocket. *It bloody must of*!

Chapter 23: Better Than Christmas

I was seriously puzzled. All the family were acting in such a buoyant mood. Nobody seemed to be caring anymore about my problems. Even Brenda shunned my attempts to gain her attention. They were still taking turns to look in on me and bring me meals, but the visits now lacked the encouragement and warmth of the previous days. The new atmosphere in the house perplexed me. Something was definitely different.

When I enquired as to what they were all playing at, the replies I received confused me more.

"Ah ha! Wouldn't you like to know?" and "You'll find out soon enough!" were the carte blanche answers. It was beginning to drive me crazy. I found it impossible to rest and no way could I concentrate on reading. Even listening to music held no pleasure and washed over my confounded pensive thoughts.

As was the routine, Mum switched off my bedroom light at ten to twelve on that Sunday evening, with her customary comment, "Good night, God bless, God bless."

The bright imposing moon shone with uncommon radiance, intruding my privacy through gaps in the badly-fitting curtains. Large distinct patterns in shadows gave my usual cosy surroundings a chilling, ghostly dimension. The old house began to settle down for the night, with its usual series of creaks and groans.

Tonight all these familiar sounds could not be easily explained and dismissed. My pulse raced to a fast drum beat. Seconds seemed like minutes, minutes seemed like hours. It wasn't until the unlikely comfort of birdsong and the room's unpleasant creepy aura was replaced with the sombre but uplifting colours of dawn breaking that my irrational fears and nervous itching began to ebb away, enabling me to close my aching eyes and rest easy.

My unwillingness to respond to nudging and prodding was causing Hilary to panic. "Wake up! Wake up!" she shouted, grabbing my shoulders sternly and vigorously shaking them. "Brian! Brian! Don't do this!"

Reluctantly my weighty eyelids flickered and begrudgingly opened.

"God, you frightened me!" exclaimed the much relieved Hilary.

She released her vice-like grip on my stretched pyjama top as I found my voice.

"What is it? What's the time?"

I rhythmically rubbed my sore eyes with the knuckles of my clenched fists.

"It's about quarter to eight," she informed me as she manoeuvred to stand tall away from the bed.

Her face couldn't contain a broad smile as she spoke. "Well, my darling brother, we've got a big surprise for you."

I was intrigued. I shifted to an upright position and waited impatiently to hear more.

Hilary tapped the side of her nose with exaggerated movements and winked. "Ahhh! Wouldn't be a surprise if I told you, would it?"

Her animated face sparkled from ear to ear.

"Who's gonna tell me then?" I enquired, frustration obvious in my squeaky voice.

"First, you've got to do something for us, otherwise you won't get it."

Hilary's announcement was relayed in such a dominant, matter-of-fact way that I just sat listening intently, not daring to argue.

"You'll get your surprise tea-time when we get home from work, but only if you get up today and have a bath and wash your hair. Do you hear me?"

"I hear you," I stammered, "but I don't understand it."

"You don't have to, just do it. I promise

you it's gonna be worth it."

She winked at me once again and left, leaving me excited, apprehensive, and very confused.

Mother's room service was just delivering a third cup of tea of the morning when I curiously reached boiling point. I spoke to concede defeat. "All right, you blackmailing lot, you win. I will have a bloody bath!"

"Language!" snapped Mum, shrugging her shoulders and grinning in her unique gummy way. "I'll light the pilot on the geezer for you then."

Hilary carefully withdrew the tea towel from around my neck, trying to keep as much of the fallen hair from dropping onto the bed. She then cautiously bent over and shook the contents of the towel into the raffia paper basket next to the sideboard. She passed me the mirror from the bedside table.

"There you are, sir. I hope it's to your liking."

I wiped dust from the glass with the flat of my hand and focused on my new image. It looked fantastic! Far better than anticipated.

I spoke with genuine gratitude. "Oh my God! That's brilliant, Hil! Thanks a million! I still don't know how you got our mum to agree to it."

"Well, there you are, and the revelations aint finished yet."

I lowered the mirror and touched the top of my head, pleased with the velvety feel of it.

Hilary shouted in the direction of the door, "Come on, you lot! Bring the pressies up."

The creaky bedroom door opened to reveal my smiling mother leading in my other two sisters, all carrying white bags bearing the famous name "Astons" in bold print on all sides. My whole body twitched with excitement.

Mum produced a trendy black Harrington jacket from her bag and ceremoniously placed it neatly next to me on the bed. "For you, sir," she announced as she backed out of the room.

It was now Brenda's turn to do her bit. She whistled loudly as she plunged her arm deep into her carrier bringing out, like a rabbit from a top hat, a bottle-green coloured pair of Stay Press trousers, still with the Levi's label dangling from them.

My face lit up the district as my eyes feasted on them.

"Pinch me, I got to be dreaming!" I hollered, scarcely able to catch my breath. I managed to croak, "Stay Press, you got me Stay Press!"

I fought back tears as Brenda copied her mother's actions and placed the desirable garment on the bed, making sure that the trouser legs were laid out straight.

Gloria fumbled clumsily into her bag she had been holding ripping it as she went. "Whoops!" she snorted, picking up the green and white gingham shirt from the bedroom mat. She held it out in front of her and shrilled, "What's think of this then, Bri? It's a Ben Sherman."

I shook my head with disbelief. "Don't know what to say," I whispered, "it's all exactly what I wanted."

"Oh, nearly forgot," exclaimed Hilary, fishing into yet another bag that she had quickly gone onto the landing to retrieve. "These should go nice with that lot," she said, placing an expensive-looking pair of heavy black brogues onto my lap.

Now that the commotion of the present frenzy was over, I was totally overwhelmed with emotion. My tears cascaded down, splashing onto the highly-polished toes of my precious new shoes. I began to feel extremely ashamed of myself. The family that over the years had never in my mind been good enough for me was now proving to me that unconditional love was mine, and love is what I should be giving back to them. I vowed that I would never again try to deny them. They were part of me and I truly cared for them. So who cares what anyone else might think of me? I would be proud of my roots and embrace rather than fight my existence.

The family looked on at my emotional response and they all wept with me. Instinctively they moved in surrounding me in a human cocoon of love.

Brenda, who had somehow taken control of events lately, asked the others to leave her alone with her distraught brother.

Before the door had even closed, a square-faced me cleared my throat with a cough. "I'm so sorry, Bren. I'll never hurt any of you ever again."

Brenda leant forward, held my hand and answered me with an assured tone, "Just be happy, Bri, you're everything to us. Just be happy."

Although embarrassment flooded through me, I had to speak from my heart: "And I love you all. I didn't know how much until today. I wouldn't swap any of you."

Brenda fumbled and brought from her cardigan pocket a badly crumpled piece of paper that had initiated all the show of affection. She handed it over for me to read. I wiped my moist cheeks and started to digest the words with a frown.

"Well what's that all about then?" I said, passing the note back to my sister.

"It was delivered on Saturday, about two minutes after Diane left."

I spoke as the penny began to drop. "So you think Diane wants me to go, is that it?"

I found it all pretty impossible to believe, but couldn't really come up with a sensible alternative.

I aimlessly twiddled with the laces of my new shoes that were beginning to dig into my legs beneath. "So that's what all this is about, is it?"

I looked searchingly into Brenda's eyes. A nervous ache was erupting deep in the pit of my stomach. On the one hand I felt that there was no way on earth that I could throw a spanner in the works and not go. I owed my generous family at least that. And yet the prospect of being launched into the outside world with all its torments chilled me. I feebly conjured one lame excuse after another why I couldn't go. I still didn't feel well enough; how could I get there anyway? I didn't want to worry Mum.

When I'd run out of ideas and steam Brenda spoke, assuring me that everything had been thought of and sorted out. I was going.

"For God's sake, Bri, you sound like our mum. Just shut up a minute and I'll tell you what the plan is."

I listened intently, trying to find the flaw in their scheme, but alas I couldn't find one.

The bedside alarm clock showed a quarter to seven. I was ready, proudly strutting around enjoying the crisp tapping sound being produced by my brogues on the lino-covered floor. I zipped my Harrington up half way, as was the style, and smirked as I gazed at myself in the mirror. *Bloody lovely!* I exclaimed approvingly.

The transformation by a pair of clippers and a new outfit was astonishing.

I casually edged over to my record player and touched a pile of records with my fingertips just for luck. I closed my eyes and took a few settling deep breaths before joining the rest of my family downstairs.

I swanked into the back room to be graciously received by my family. They all sat eagerly awaiting the first glimpse of Brian Wilson Mark II. They nearly burst with pride as they studied the smart young man that stood before them. I majestically turned a full circle and smiled with an air of arrogance.

Mother fought her way out of her chair to kiss me with unfamiliar tenderness on both of my cheeks. For the very first time I didn't feel annoyed by her slobbering and enjoyed the moment. My new-found reaction was a catalyst for the rest of my audience to show a spontaneous admiration for their new grown-up brother. They applauded and whistled loudly before bestowing on me heartfelt compliments.

"You look so handsome!" shouted Gloria.

"Not 'alf!" agreed Brenda, not being able to resist a touch of my immaculate shiny jacket.

"You'll knock 'em dead," said Hilary.

"I bloody hope not!" I replied with a broad, confident smile, adding to my new man-about-town image.

Brenda stood up and took me by the arm. "Come on, good looking, Jim's outside ready to take you."

She led me cautiously out of the house, with the rest of the throng close behind.

I shivered as I came into contact with the bitterly cold air of the night, turned and waved dramatically to the four plump figures that stifled the house lights from reaching the outside world. I could still make out their silhouettes, elbowing and nudging each other as they jostled for position in the doorway, as Jim pulled away taking me on my journey to Southleaze School.

Chapter 24: Wonderful World

The butterflies in my stomach were the size of pigeons as we drew up beside the high red wall that encased the vast school grounds.

Jim looked across and saw my gaunt, sallow expression. He leant over my lap and flipped the door handle. It swung open with a low graunching whine.

"Go on then, Brian, go and enjoy yourself. You got nothin' to worry about. I'll pick you up at ten o'clock."

I stammered, "I don't think I can, Jim, my knees won't stop knocking."

"Well I aint takin' you back home, son," grinned Jim, "they'd bloody lynch me!"

I gave a brave smile before swinging my legs round and pulling myself up and out of the car.

"Good luck!" shouted Jim as he manoeuvred to slam the passenger door from his driver's seat.

The confidence that the last few hours had produced drained away in a split second. My voyage of self-discovery had now reached an abrupt dead end. Reality was now turning me back into a cold, frightened, vulnerable boy. I quaked as I watched the smoke from Jim's exhaust glide up and disappear and it met the amber glow of the tall streetlights. Fear gripped me like a vice. I wished I could run, but all directions looked as daunting as the other.

I turned facing the gates of the school and beyond them, thirty yards along the driveway, stood the shadowy building that was periodically being brightened by illuminated flashes of colour as moving disco lights danced across the assembly hall windows.

I lacked any enthusiasm for socialising – I was far too scared. Yet some unexplainable reflex, as a moth to a flame, was magnetically drawing me in, insisting that I move towards the only semblance of civilisation that was on offer.

As I approached, the rhythmic bumping beat of the music met my ears. I gladly left the scary barren atmosphere of night and entered the warmth of the school reception area. The windows and door to the adjoining hall looked strangely out of place as black crêpe paper precariously hung over them, acting as a blackout for the party beyond.

The one in a million chance that Diane Lewis might be already inside waiting for me urged me on, giving me renewed strength and a determination to see what lay behind the large paper-clad door.

I carefully leant my weight onto the assembly hall door, allowing it to open just wide enough for me to slip "Eel-like" inside, into the total blackness. I backed onto the door until they clunked shut behind me.

The pitch-black hall was a commotion of noise as loud tinny music mixed with raised voices and raucous screaming, that was being emitted from the faceless forms, that darted around in all directions.

My eyes slowly accustomed themselves to the very limited light source. I squinted, straining to survey the makeshift discotheque that lay before me.

Then, suddenly, the music switched to a deafening faster beat and from the stage to the side of me the do-it-yourself light show commenced. Three huge light bulbs – red, blue and green – were somehow fixed to the ends of long wooden poles and propelled around from a central pivot that sat precariously on top of a monstrous-looking electric motor. The arms of this invention moved with a slow jerky uncertainty that brought a wry smile to my lips. Instead of transforming the room into a temple of enjoyment, it created the distinct impression of a prisoner of war camp with a watchtower and spotlight, occasionally blinding you as the turning light bounced on you, only to quickly

163

be gone and leave you scrabbling once again in the obscure darkness.

I traced the path of the bright red light as it reluctantly moved at eye level around the large hall. As the five- hundred watt illumination neared the far wall, for a split second the distinct figure of Diane Lewis was quite visible. Then, blackness, and she was gone again from view. I urged the light to quicken its circuit, just to satisfy myself that it was her and this time, as it reached the same area, no one was there, she was gone. My spirits plummeted. I shuffled my feet restlessly, scanning the room frantically, desperately attempting to locate my sweetheart.

I moved away from the entrance doors and mingled aimlessly with the marauding teenagers. All were buoyantly letting off steam, boisterously enjoying themselves. No one seemed to notice me. I felt quite invisible from their façade of happiness.

I painstakingly covered every inch of the floor in a despairing hunt for Diane. My pursuit was becoming more and more desperate as emotions once again started to envelope me. The incessant music seemed to grow louder and louder. The annoying coloured lights, although intended for pleasure, now seemed to spear into my soul as they unmercifully flashed into my searing wide eyes. My head swam feverishly as panic overcame me. The whole scene of music, lights, laughter and mayhem was now taking on a macabre, disturbing complexity.

I had to get out, and quick.

Self-preservation and instinct guided my frantic stumbling towards the door. In a blink I was out, released from the unpleasantness and back into a calmer, more tolerable environment. I departed unsteadily. I peered out of the school into the gloomy, foreboding night. The bitterly cold breeze bit into my face as it made contact with my clammy, wet cheeks. I supported my limp, agitated body by gripping tightly to the wood-stained fire doors as I wearily edged myself from the building. My pulse still raced through my skull. My eyes and ears still fought to reject the sights and sounds that had just bombarded them.

I found myself once again filling my lungs fully through my nose, striving to regulate my heightened senses, wanting to again discover the person that my family had helped to produce earlier that day.

My wrist watch revealed another problem. *Oh shit!* I sighed as I pondered. *It's only five past eight.* I had nearly two hours before my lift would arrive and get me away from this misery. What could I do? *I know*, I thought, remembering the money that Mum had given me earlier as I was leaving the house. *I'll get the bus. I can be home before Jim comes out.*

I strode purposefully along the driveway towards the gates, enjoying the echoing clip-clop of the leather soled brogues as they connected with the concrete path. I instinctively slowed my pace as I neared the outer wall of the school grounds. I knew Diane Lewis was in there. I still wanted her, but not like this, not in that ridiculous pretence that was supposed to be a fun evening.

I glanced back at the structure that I had just escaped from. I shook my irrational head at what I could see, for standing waving to me from the school doorway was a beaming Diane Lewis.

Just as I began to raise my own arm to acknowledge her actions, a chilling, blood-curdling noise rose up, drilling through me. It was the unmistakable rasping noise of scooters drawing near. The rhythmic high-pitched clacking that had haunted my recent dreams, evoking terror and fear to sicken me to the core. I was glued helpless to the spot, feeling the familiar terrifying vulnerability. The high-pitched squeal of brakes brought my senses to full alert as Kuzeki and Hardy skilfully halted their machines at either side of me. I quaked violently, frightened of inciting any confrontation. I automatically lowered my head as if in the presence of royalty.

Hardy shouted loudly, making himself heard over the revving of their cherished Lambrettas, "Oy, kid! Get over 'ere!"

My chest tightened, shortening my already spasmodic breathing. I feared the worst as I slowly advanced towards the ominous figures sitting proudly on their imposing means of transport.

Cautiously I lifted my head, looking directly into the demonic face of the evil Dean Hardy. A cold shudder etched its way from the top to the bottom of my perspiration-saturated back. Hardy's slanted grin hung like an arrogant accessory on his hound dog features.

He spoke with a sharpness straight into my upturned sallow face. "You could have grassed on us to the law."

The rancid stench of stale tobacco and sour alcohol violated my nostrils. I fought to control the feeling of nausea and retching that welled up within me.

The unpredictable bully spoke again with a cold, heartless edge in his voice. "Look at you, all dressed up! Proper little Mod, aint you?"

His accomplice butted in. "Fair play to you,

kid. You didn't grass on us. We think a lot of that."

"Certainly do," snarled Hardy, scratching his face roughly.

"If you ever want anythin', let us know. You're all right."

I managed a jittery smile and nodded respectfully to both of them.

They carefully steered their scooters to face away from me and then, with an exaggerated twist of the handlebar throttles, screeched away, leaving a rising pungent cloud of grey exhaust fumes to float up into the atmosphere.

Bewildered and immensely relieved, I slumped back, leaning heavily onto the brick wall behind me.

The turmoil of mixed emotions jammed my nervous system. My re-emergence back into society had been fraught with dramatic events. I attempted to hoist myself to a standing position, only to collapse back once again. My energy levels were severely depleted. The emotions of the last few minutes were taking their toll. My legs felt like jelly, unable to fully support my distressed and tormented mood. Time inevitably began to heal my distraught emotions.

I glanced across to the grass verge, just off to my right. At the far end stood a rotten, graffiti-splattered bench. It looked inviting as a safe haven for me to rest my distraught and listless frame. With a rejuvenated boost I managed to peel myself away from the wall that supported me. Then, after a toddler-like stagger and stumble along the uneven pavement, I manoeuvred myself and dropped with an ungainly bump onto the slatted wooden seat. I cradled my troubled head with my upturned hands and rocked involuntarily. My battle-weary senses were now beginning to show signs of returning to a functional state. My fear-ridden thoughts were becoming less foreboding and my tired body was returning to a less threatened level. I closed my eyes and pondered on the extraordinary events of my day.

As I wrestled with my befuddled brain, I noticed a dark shadow fall across my hunched figure. My heart jumped. *Oh no! They have changed their minds . . . they've come back for me!*

The soft melodic voice of Diane brought me fully back to reality. As she spoke she tenderly placed a hand on my shoulder.

"Brian, are you okay? What did those troublemakers want with you?"

I lifted my head and looked straight into her beautiful blue eyes that still shone like beacons on this cold, damp night. Her warm smile was rescuing me from my anxiety and the feelings of intimidation.

I spoke, returning her soft tone. "They wanted to thank me for not telling on them. There's a turn up, eh?"

As I finished with a strained smile, Diane purposefully turned and sat next to me, pressing herself comfortingly against me. "I haven't had chance to tell you how handsome you look in all your new gear, or how much I liked your family."

As she finished she leant towards me and gently kissed me on the cheek. The feel of her warm, moist lips sent a tremor of pleasure right down to my toes.

I looked at her and negotiated a reply. "Thank you, Diane, thank you for everything."

We gazed once more into each other's eyes. The world seemed to drift into insignificance. Nothing mattered at all, other than the precious girl by my side.

Diane broke the spell that engulfed me with her voice. "Well, can we go back to the disco so I can show off my boyfriend?"

The word boyfriend made me tingle with delight. *Is that I what I am? Her boyfriend?*

We both stood up simultaneously and started to stroll towards the vibrant lights that were still etching their uncertain forms across the shroud of darkness.

With the confident air of a seasoned Romeo, I took Diane's petite, elegant hand into mine. She accepted it willingly, moved closer to me and nuzzled her nose and face into my upper arm. We mooched along totally at one with each other's company. For the first time in my topsy-turvy life a rush of extreme contentment occupied my consciousness. I now could see the world with a new refreshing optimism. The love for Diane, that was now being clearly reciprocated, was making me float like a bird ten feet above the pavement. I could hardly contain myself from screaming out with excitement.

I also reflected on the kind and selfless actions of my sisters and mother in getting me to this point. A strong sense of guilt played on me as I recounted the many times I had been ashamed or embarrassed by them in the past.

My family's expression of love for me could now be fully understood. Never, ever would I try to hurt or humiliate them again. They are mine and I love them.

As we neared the school building, our footsteps became shorter. As we gazed tenderly at each other, wallowing in each other's companionship, Diane slipped her arms cleverly through mine and drew me close. She laid her head gently in the nape of my neck and we hugged each other affectionately.

I smiled as I placed a loving kiss onto the top of her immaculate blonde head.

Tears of joy began to roll down my satisfied cheeks.

These really were the tears of a clown.

Lightning Source UK Ltd.
Milton Keynes UK
UKOW04f0813220917
309681UK00001B/3/P

9 781787 195295